Smith's MONTHLY

Every Month Original Novels, Stories, and Articles

USA Today Bestselling Writer
Dean Wesley Smith

TABLE OF CONTENTS

SHORT STORIES

FULL NOVEL

SERIAL NOVEL

NONFICTION

Smith's Monthly Issue #17

The Writings and Opinions of

Dean Wesley Smith

Introduction
WELCOME TO PATREON SUPPORTERS

IN THE BACK of this issue you might notice a list of names. Walter White Cat and I are thanking those wonderful people for being supporters of my blog, my writing, and this magazine through the website called Patreon.

For those of you who don't read my blog regularly, Walter White Cat is my cat who sticks with me all the time and naps with me. In fact, as I write this, he is sleeping on my other chair here in my office.

Patreon is a wonderful way for patrons of the arts to donate a small amount per month to an artist or a project such as this one. Lots of musicians, graphic artists, comic book artists, and writers have accounts on Patreon that allow others to support the artist or writer's work.

Throughout the country, many, many artists are managing to chase their dreams thanks to wonderful support from people such as the ones thanked in the back of this issue.

Also, many of the Patreon supporters are getting an issue for the first time. So for those of you new here, welcome to the craziness.

In this issue is a full Thunder Mountain novel, four short stories, and the last chapters of a Poker Boy short novel serial.

Starting next issue will be even more fun stuff, including some nonfiction. Plus a new novel and more short stories.

Every issue tends to be a surprise.

All sixteen of the previous issues are still available for sale in local bookstores and online in both paper and electronic editions. All sixteen have a full original novel in them, plus short stories, serials, some nonfiction, and even a few poems.

So welcome, Patreon supporters to this crazy project. I hope you enjoy it.

I know your support, and the support of the subscribers to this magazine, mean

Thanks for the Support

Dean Wesley Smith

a lot to me. More than I can ever express as a writer.

I just hope I keep you entertained with the stories and novels. And that you want to keep coming back for more stories.

Thanks, everyone.
Now onward.

—Dean Wesley Smith
February 1st, 2015
Lincoln City, Oregon

#1... October 2013

#2... November 2013

#3... December 2013

#4... January 2014

#5... February 2014

#6... March 2014

#7... April 2014

#8... May 2014

#9... June 2014

#10... July 2014

#11... August 2014

#12...September 2014

#13... October 2014

#14... November 2014

#15... December 2014

#16...January 2015

Coming Next Issue in Smith's Monthly
A return to the Cold Poker Gang Mystery Series in a brand new novel.

CALLING DEAD

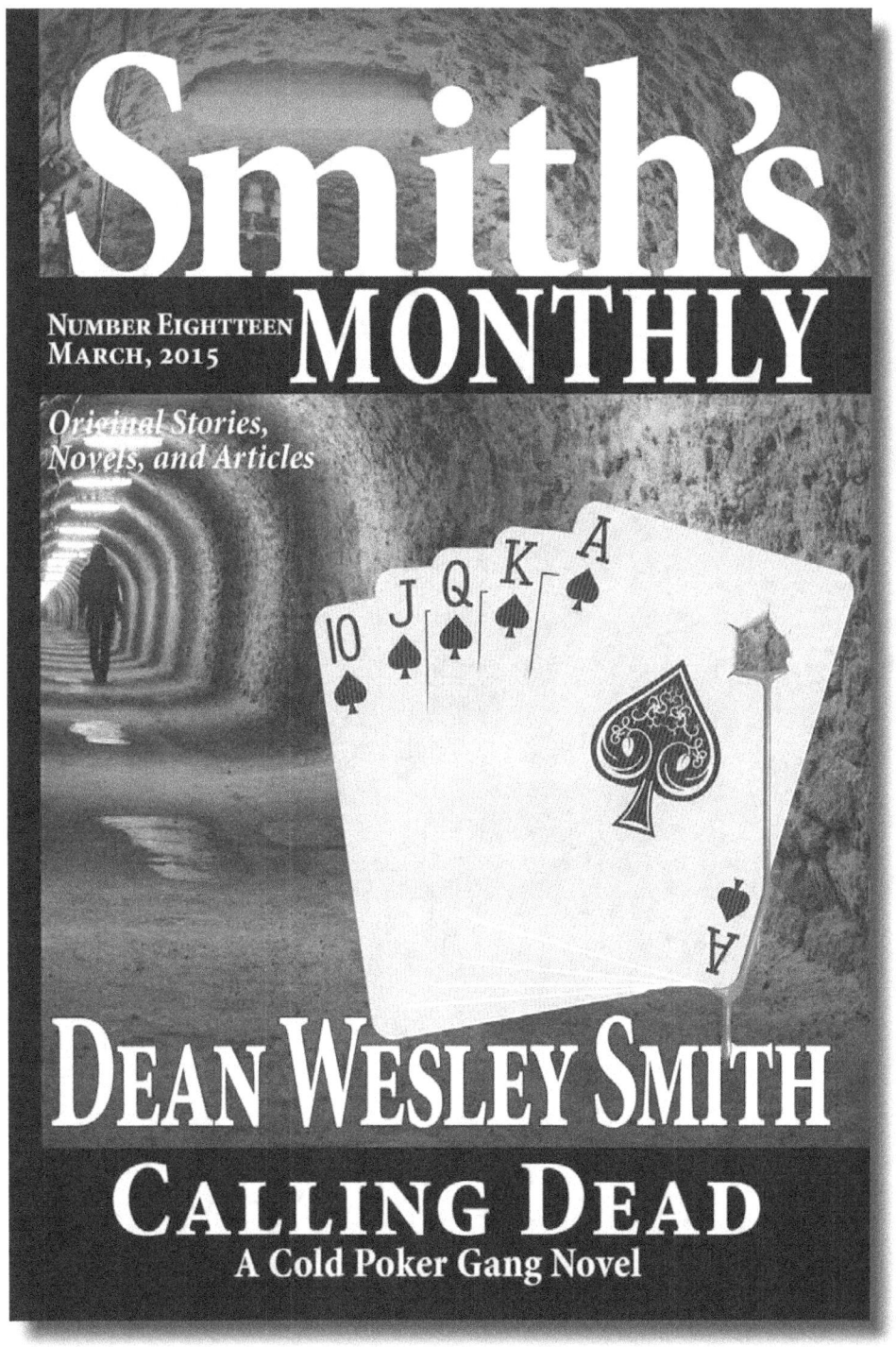

Smith's MONTHLY

NUMBER EIGHTTEEN
MARCH, 2015

Original Stories, Novels, and Articles

DEAN WESLEY SMITH

CALLING DEAD
A Cold Poker Gang Novel

Dean Wesley Smith

USA Today Bestselling Writer

THE Empty Mummy Murders

A POKER BOY STORY

For the second time in his life, Poker Boy finds himself trying to help a woman stalked by the alien-looking Silicon Suckers.

He failed the first time and they killed an old girlfriend of his.

This time the Silicon Suckers have killed three other women. Can he save the woman asking for help and more importantly help her save herself?

THE EMPTY MUMMY MURDERS
A Poker Boy Story

ONE

IT WAS A GOOD ten minutes into the conversation over vanilla milkshakes and a side of fries with Scary Mary, as her friends called her and she called herself, before she got to the point.

Scary Mary deserved the name. She had bright red hair tied up so tight on the top of her head that it pulled the skin of her face and scalp upward. She wore more makeup than a bad rodeo clown, and had breasts that must have arrived at the restaurant a good minute ahead of her.

Her tight red dress, if you could call the small piece of cloth covering her largest assets a dress, I'm sure didn't cover her butt when she slid into the leather booth at The Diner. But I didn't look. In Vegas you saw all types, and a long time ago I had learned to not judge a person by their look or a woman by the expanded size of her chest.

Some friend-of-a-friend had given Scary Mary one of my real-world names and told her I might be able to help with her problems.

As Poker Boy, I find people to help in all sorts of ways. Sometimes I find them, sometimes they come to me, sometimes my boss, Stan the God of Poker, assigns me the task of helping someone. It never seems to make any sense how I find the people who need saving, but I do. Just as I find the people at poker tables who need me to take their money. It seems to be a natural way of the world.

I had told Scary Mary to meet me at The Diner in downtown Las Vegas. The Diner serves the best milkshakes on the planet, and the waitress who is always there is Madge, a superhero in the food service business. The Diner is decorated like a fake 1960s diner. I am convinced there were no places in the 1960s that looked anything like The Diner, with re-cords stapled on the walls and photos of Elvis, Marilyn, and James Dean on most walls.

But the booths were comfortable and the milkshakes huge and made like old milkshakes from the 1930s. And it was where my team met when we had a job to plan.

It was two in the afternoon. No one but Madge was with us in The Diner, and she was working up behind the counter. Scary Mary and I were in a booth near the front door. It was a perfect time to get to the bottom of her problem.

Scary Mary kept looking at me in a worried fashion, so I sort of turned on my Trust-Me power and let it wash over her. I had on my black leather jacket and black fedora-like hat that was my superhero uniform, and I could feel the power they gave me drawing from the nearby casi-nos. It should be more than enough to get Scary Mary to talk.

After a moment she blushed, which looked washed-out next to her blazing-red hair and beside her thick, blue eyeliner and red lipstick.

"You're not going to believe me and I just don't know what you can do to help," she said, her voice deep and throaty.

"Try me," I said, turning up my Trust-Me" power a little and adding a little Empathy power to it as well. "You would be surprised at what I might be able to do."

"That's what my friend in the poker room at the MGM told me. But you just won't believe me."

"Let me decide that," I said.

She signed, looked both directions. "I'm being harassed by aliens."

"Oh, no," I said, sighing and stirring up my milkshake. This felt like a problem I had had three years before with an old girlfriend. She hadn't let me help her and she had ended up dead.

"I told you that you wouldn't believe me," Scary Mary said, clearly disgusted.

"Oh, I believe you," I said. "The aliens you are seeing have large heads, big eyes, and are gray. Right?"

"Yes, yes," she said, jumping a little in the booth in excitement and almost knocking over her milkshake with the large extensions on her chest.

I sighed again. "Those aren't aliens. Those are creatures called Silicon Suckers. And my bet is they are after your breasts."

Both her hands went to cover a few inches of the mass on her chest, her eyes wide, her mouth open.

Silicon Suckers are the reason the UFO nuts think there are aliens visiting earth. They have big oblong heads with long thin excuses for chins. Their bodies are thin, humanoid, but all gray in color. Their feet are huge and they walk like they are floating through the air without a sound. And they have lived in their caves in the deserts for far longer than there have been humans around.

What drives me nuts about them are their huge eyes. They don't seem to blink, and that can just unnerve a guy, even me, a superhero.

They have no smell, but can suck moisture out of an area faster than a hundred dehumidifiers on full blast. And for some stupid reason, of all the people and superheroes and gods that exist, I am the one who has become the go-to-guy for dealing with the Silicon Suckers.

I keep wanting to tell people I play poker for a living, I work for Stan, the God of Poker, and I do my best work in casinos helping people who come into poker rooms solve their problems. As far as I know, Silicon Suckers don't even know what poker is.

Now here I was again, talking to a woman who needed help with the Silicon Suckers. If this trend didn't stop, I might start being called Silicon Sucker Boy. And I would hate that.

"So what have they been doing?" I asked, dreading the answer.

She still had her hands firmly planted over small areas of her massive breasts.

"What do you mean they might be after my breasts?"

"First tell me what they are doing," I said, sending as much Calming Power as I could generate her way. I wasn't in that good of control of that superpower yet, but by simply trying to calm a person, I sometimes could.

She took a deep breath and then nodded. "I first saw them in the parking garage off my apartment, out near the airport. They just stood there, staring at me."

"Two of them?"

"Yeah," she said. "At first I figured them for nutcases from a convention, but they are very skinny and I couldn't see costumes.

"You've seen them more times?"

She nodded. "A couple of dozen times and twice they got into my apartment. Made the place so dry I was afraid it was going to burst into flames."

"Silicon Suckers live under the desert and take moisture out of the air," I said, nodding. "Have they tried to touch you?"

"No," she said, shaking her head and shivering.

I stared into her worried eyes and knew I was way out of my depth. Any question I might have next about changes to her chest would sound bad coming from me. I needed some help.

"Hold on just a minute, would you?" I asked. "I want to call a friend to make sure there haven't been any other sightings lately."

She nodded and I motioned for Madge to come over as I stood.

"You interested in a hamburger?" I asked Scary Mary. "On me."

She nodded and I turned to Madge who had heard me. "My normal burger, one for Mary, and a shake and burger for Patty as well. I'll be right back."

Madge nodded. She would entertain Scary Mary until I got back with Patty. With luck, it would only be a minute.

TWO

I STEPPED outside the door into the warm fall day, then jumped to a spot in front of the MGM Grand main hotel lobby check-in desk. Then, before a camera could pick up my sudden appearance, I pulled myself and Patty out of the flow of time.

I loved being able to teleport, and even more being able to stop time. Actually, I couldn't stop time but it looked like I could. I actually just could step between moments in time. And I could take others with me into that moment, which made everyone else look frozen around me.

My girlfriend, Patty Ledgerwood, aka Front Desk Girl, had just finishing checking in a woman with two kids. The woman and the two kids were frozen in place moving away from the counter and Patty was smiling at me.

"Thank you," she said. "I needed a break."

"My pleasure," I said, smiling back. Just seeing Patty always made me smile. She had long brown hair that she had tied back while working. Her wonderful brown eyes were deep enough for me to get lost in and I had many, many times. Today she had on a white blouse and black slacks and a light tan MGM jacket that was the uniform of the day. She looked good in anything, but I was in love with her, so my opinion was clearly not one anyone could trust.

"So what's happening?"

"I need some help with a woman who's being visited by Silicon Suckers," I said.

"Oh, oh," Patty said. "Does she…?"

"Bigger than I thought possible," I said, indicating how large Scary Mary's breasts were.

"And you want me to help you question her about them?"

"I screwed this up once," I said. "I'd kind of like to get it right if her breasts are the problem."

Patty knew about my old girlfriend and how she had refused to give back her breast implants made out of silicon from a sacred Silicon Sucker's burial ground. The Silicon Suckers had eventually removed the breasts through her ass, for some reason the only way they know of to get inside a human body, and it had killed her.

Failing to save her always felt like one of my biggest mistakes.

Patty nodded. "Meet me in the hallway down near my car. I'll be right there."

I nodded and jumped to that spot while also stepping back into the flow of time. In Vegas a person couldn't just jump around through space without also being careful to not be picked up on cameras. Patty and I had a regular camera dead spot.

It took Patty exactly four minutes to get off work and meet me. Her boss at the MGM Grand knew what she did and that sometimes she just needed some time away. In fact, her boss was another super-hero working the same area.

I jumped us out of there the moment Patty hit the camera safe area and back to a spot just in front of The Diner.

I led the way inside, telling Patty what I had ordered her. Madge was just heading back to the kitchen and Scary Mary was sitting nervously in the booth twisting the straw in her milkshake. Clearly Madge had stood and talked with her for a few minutes while I was gone.

I introduced Patty to Scary Mary and then said, "Patty knows all about the Silicon Suckers."

Patty nodded as Scary Mary sort of beamed behind all the makeup.

"I've seen them a number of times," Patty said. "And even been down in one of the caves they call sand castles."

"Wow," Scary Mary said. "I thought for sure I was going insane."

"Far from it," Patty said. "But these creatures are very dangerous, and we need to try to figure out what changed for you that started them visiting you."

"That way we have a chance of stopping them," I said.

Scary Mary nodded and I hit her again with another wave of my Relax and Trust-Me super power. She seemed to calm a little more.

Patty, who was sitting beside me in the booth, patted my leg and then leaned toward Scary Mary. "So what day exactly did you first see the Silicon Suckers?"

Scary Mary twisted her face and layered makeup around, clearly trying to think, then said, "May sixteenth."

"So, anything major happen the week before that?" Patty asked. "Anything change?"

"I got a new job," Scary Mary said without hesitation. "Five days before. I remember because it was May Eleventh, one year from the day exactly that I had my sex change operation, and I figured that was a good sign."

So Scary Mary used to be Scary Martin, but I doubted that was going to have anything to do with this case. Patty clearly didn't either because she said nothing. Again, this was Vegas. We had seen most everything.

"What was your new job?" Patty asked.

"Dispatcher," she said. "Desert High Sand and Gravel. I used to drive a truck, but after my operation Ben, the owner, said that once I got recovered, he'd find a place for me. And he did."

"What happened to the previous dispatcher?" I asked, afraid of the answer.

"Sharon? She vanished one day," Scary Mary said. "No sign of her but her ex-husband was knocking her around at one point so they're looking at him."

Patty sighed and looked down.

I would bet anything that the previous dispatcher had been killed by the Silicon Suckers. But it would never be proved. Somewhere, at some point, the trucks that Scary Mary was sending out were doing something to anger the Silicon Suckers. And since she sent them out, they were blaming her. And clearly they'd blamed the woman who had her job ahead of her.

Then Patty asked a question I hadn't thought to ask.

"Did any other dispatchers disappear besides Sharon?"

"Joyce," Scary Mary said. "And there might have been another, but I'm not sure."

Then, suddenly she realized where we were going. "You don't think that these aliens caused them to vanish?"

Both Patty and I nodded and Scary Mary turned white under all the makeup.

THREE

MADGE BROUGHT the food at that point, and it gave me a chance to think. My entire premise that the Silicon Suckers were after Scary Mary's breasts had gone out the window. Most of the time I dealt with the Silicon Suckers because of land problems. They were very, very protective of their land, and had negotiated with the gods, including Lady Luck herself, a compromise that allowed humans to build Las Vegas. But with the recent expansion, there had been many dust-ups lately over land.

This was looking like another one of those. And clearly the Silicon Suckers were warning each dispatcher in their own way, giving them time to stop, then killing them when they didn't and starting over with a new dispatcher.

Scary Mary had had no idea her job was so deadly when she took it.

After Madge put down the wonderful-smelling hamburgers and fries and left, I started to quiz Scary Mary about the business as we ate.

Turns out the company only had one large sand quarry in the desert outside of town. And the first mile of road from the pit was gravel across desert as well.

Scary Mary's job was to dispatch the trucks full of gravel or sand from the quarry to different jobs around the city or concrete mixing plants. She had to keep track of forty trucks, but in the boom times the dispatcher had managed over a hundred and had them on the go constantly for two shifts a day. She said she used to drive one of those trucks.

"I need maps of the quarry and the road in and out of it," I said. "And then I'll compare them to Silicon Sucker lands."

I took a big bite of my hamburger, then stood. "It won't take long," I said.

I headed out the door, and the moment I was on the sidewalk and the young couple walking toward Freemont Street had their back turned, I shouted to the air, "Stan. Need help in your office."

Since I didn't have an office and I didn't want Scary Mary to know what I could really do, I figured Stan's office would be as good as any.

A moment later I found myself in a standard business office and Stan in his normal black slacks and tan shirt stood facing me beside an oak desk with a computer and chair. A couple plants filled the corners and the windows looked out over Vegas from high in the air. Far higher than any office building.

"I got to teach you how to build your-self an office when you need it," he said, shaking his head.

"I can do this?" I asked, stunned, looking around at the furniture and the fantastic view of the invisible floating office. I had always figured that only the gods could build offices.

Stan just shook his head in slight disgust and then said, "What do you need?"

I told him which maps I needed and a moment later they appeared in the air, the map of the Silicon Sucker lands floating on one side, the map of the quarry and road on the other.

"You going to tell me why you need these two maps?" he asked.

"Just put them at the same scale and overlay them," I said. "We just might see why."

He did, the two maps floating until they merged. The quarry was a long ways from the Silicon Sucker land, but the road was another matter.

"There," I said, pointing to one area where the road seemed to touch the Silicon Sucker's land. "Can you make that larger?"

The road clearly had been laid out to go around a corner of the Silicon Sucker's land, making a ninety-degree corner.

I was betting that corner had been cut off. And people had been dying because of it.

I glanced around. "Can you put us and this office right over that corner?"

An instant later we were over the cor-ner of the dirt road, floating in the air still inside the office, only now part of the of-fice floor under our feet was invisible.

That felt kind of creepy and cool at the same time. I really needed to learn how to do all this.

Below, I could still see the old road, but clearly a new one had been construct-ed a few years back that cut directly across Silicon Sucker land. More than likely the owner just figured it was desert land and no one would care. As we watched, float-ing invisible in an air-conditioned office above, a truck full of gravel powered through the corner leaving a trail of dust.

"Oh, shit," Stan said.

"The Suckers have been warning and then killing the truck dispatchers," I said. "Blaming them for sending the trucks across their lands. The newest one came to me because she thought she was seeing aliens."

"It was worse," Stan said.

Then something on the old road caught my eye and I could feel my stom-ach drop. I wished I hadn't had that bite of hamburger.

"Hang on," I said and teleported to the old section of road.

The heat of the desert hit me hard and it was a moderately cool day in the fall. I couldn't imagine how hot it was out here in the summer.

Right square in the middle of the road was a long mound of sand built crosswise to the road. Beside that were two others.

"Oh, don't tell me," Stan said, appearing beside me.

I eased over and carefully moved a little sand on one pile with my shoe, just enough to uncover the mummified remains of a human hand, drained of all moisture.

"Shit!" Stan said.

All I wanted to do was be sick. I stepped back and tried to take a deep breath of the hot air, but that didn't help much.

FOUR

"WHERE IS THE WOMAN you are helping now?" Stan asked, also still staring at the three mounds clearly covering three bodies. He was the God of Poker and been around for thousands of years. And I was a superhero. That didn't mean that we had gotten used to things like this. You could never get used to this kind of thing. Ever.

"She's with Patty and Madge at The Diner," I said.

"Let's go there and figure this out," Stan said.

"Scary Mary doesn't know who we are or what we can do," I said.

Stan shook his head. "She's going to know now."

We jumped back to the booth and Scary Mary jumped so hard against the back of the booth, her large breasts just about hit her in the forehead.

Patty looked shocked as I slid in beside her and took a long drink from a glass of water. Stan pulled up a chair and took another glass of water and drank it.

Then he reached across the table and extended his hand. "I'm Stan."

"Mary," she said, taking his hand carefully. "People call me Scary Mary. And how did you do that?"

"There's a reason you came to us for help," Stan said. "Just trust us."

She nodded and said nothing, but I could tell she wanted to bolt for the door. Seeing aliens was one thing, seeing two men appear out of thin air was another.

"This has to be bad," Patty said, "or you wouldn't have come in like that."

"Very bad," I said. Then with Madge listening, I explained about the corner

and what we had found on the old unused part of the road.

Mary now looked like she would be sick. "I drove for two of them," she said. "How is this possible?"

"Silicon Suckers are very, very protective of their land," I said. "They consider what they have been doing with you a warning to stop sending trucks over their land. They must have done the same thing with the other three."

"But you said they might be after my breasts," Scary Mary said.

"My first assumption; I was wrong," I said. "I had an old friend who ended up with silicon breast enhancements that were made from a sacred Silicon Sucker burial ground. She wouldn't give them back, so the Silicon Suckers took them."

"But the issue this time is the road and that shortcut," Stan said. "You said you used to drive for this company?"

"Before my operation," Scary Mary said. "A bunch of drivers built the shortcut across that corner back in the boom times, when we were all in such a hurry to do as many loads as possible. God, such a stupid thing to kill three women over."

"Not to the Silicon Suckers," Patty said. "All their land is very sacred."

"Poker Boy," Stan said, "you deal with the Silicon Suckers more than anyone. Any idea what we need to do now?"

I honestly had no idea. There were three bodies on the old road that the police were going to need to do something with. And more than likely that would be a crime scene for some time. If the trucks kept using that shortcut, Scary Mary wouldn't live very long.

I turned to Scary Mary who was looking shocked and puzzled, or at least that's how I thought she was looking under the layers of makeup. Clearly sex-change operations didn't come with lessons in makeup.

"Is there another way in and out of that quarry?"

"South toward the freeway and then into town past the airport," she said.

"That's directly away from Silicon Sucker land," Stan said, nodding. "I'll get the police on the bodies and work with Laverne to talk with the Gods of Land Use to get permission to use the road past the Silicon Sucker lands revoked."

I nodded. Stan would take care of the surface problems. My problem still sat across from me.

"Good luck," he said. Then with a nod to Scary Mary, he vanished.

"How…how…how…?"

Scary Mary just kept staring at where he had been.

I tried one of my French Fries, but it just no longer tasted good. Somehow I still had to figure out a way to save Scary Mary's life. We would get the trucks stopped, but I had a hunch Scary Mary had insulted the Silicon Suckers for just too long a time. She would need to apologize or end up dead.

Finally Scary Mary moved her attention from the vanishing Stan to the quiet that rested over the table. She looked at Patty, then at me. "I'm still in danger, aren't I?"

Patty nodded. "I'm afraid so. But give us a little time. We'll protect you until we can get something figured out."

"Think fast," Madge said as two Silicon Suckers appeared near the door and the air in the restaurant got suddenly very, very dry.

FIVE

I DIDN'T KNOW they could teleport. That explained a great deal.

I stood and stepped toward the two alien-looking creatures. Then in their language of clicks and snaps and grunts, I said, "It is an honor to be in the presence of such great beings."

"Thank you, Poker Boy," the one on the right said in clear English without seeming to move his lips. "The honor is ours. Today you visited the great scar in our lands."

"Yes, I did not know about it until today," I said, having no idea what to say but the truth. "I have become very upset at such an insult to my wonderful friends, the Silicon Suckers. The human vehicles that crossed across your sacred lands and damaged them are being stopped and will not come near your lands again. The humans must retrieve the dead that caused such damage, but then that path near your sacred lands will be closed completely."

The restaurant was becoming tinder dry and Patty and Scary Mary sat perfectly still in the booth. Madge stood near her counter, also not moving.

"When will this ceremony take place?" the Silicon Sucker asked.

I had no idea what he meant by ceremony, but with that corner being a crime scene, we wouldn't be able to do anything there anytime soon. I bowed slightly. "May we beg for one half of a moon cycle to prepare and for the humans to finish removing their dead?"

The Silicon Sucker bowed slightly, then said, "Yes, that will be acceptable."

I had just bought us and Scary Mary two weeks. I hoped that would be enough time.

Then the Silicon Sucker turned and looked at Scary Mary for a moment, then back at me. If they stepped toward her, there would be nothing I could do to stop them that wouldn't insult them deeply and maybe cause a war between the gods and Silicon Suckers. So far, in my understanding, there had only been two such wars throughout all time. Both fought over land.

Scary Mary had damaged their land in their minds. No god or superhero could or would stop them if they wanted to take her.

"Will the human that sent such machines over our land be at the ceremony?"

"She did not understand what she was doing until she received your warnings and came to me. She is disgusted at her carelessness, and is the reason it is stopping now. She will bow in great respect and offer herself and her gifts in hopes the great Silicon Suckers will allow her to live."

He bowed slightly again and then said, "We will be watching."

"It was an honor as always," I said, bowing to them.

Both bowed in return and then vanished.

"Open the door and let some moisture in here," Madge said after a moment.

I did as I was told and then went back to the booth and drank three glasses of the water that Madge brought.

We had two weeks to save Scary Mary's life.

SIX

WE FAILED.

That afternoon at The Diner we tried our best to convince Scary Mary to keep her mouth shut about the murders and what she knew. And never say anything about the Silicon Suckers, but it ended up under questioning she didn't remain quiet.

Or couldn't. I never knew.

The murders hit the headlines, of course. When it became known that the corpses had been hollowed out, with most of the insides pulled out of the victims' asses, it got even more sensational. The press called them the "Empty Mummy Murders."

I didn't want to mention to the press that most mummies were empty.

After the police were done, Stan got the Gods of Land Use to go in and close off and destroy any sign of any road across the Silicon Suckers land, and even had them replant new desert grass and weeds.

Two major rocks were placed at both ends of the old shortcut to make sure no one went out there over the Silicon Sucker land.

And, of course, the road to the crime scene was closed off completely from the quarry to the location of the bodies and also from the highway to the location at the corner.

But Scary Mary just couldn't keep her mouth shut. She started insisting that it was aliens who had killed the women. And that there were people in The Diner who could appear and disappear.

That sounded totally insane, so the police started investigating her past and

her sanity and came up will all sorts of things that didn't look good besides her makeup.

Scary Mary was tossed into custody not only as a suspect in the murders, but also for other events that happened in her past, including the accidental drowning in a pool of Scary Mary's first wife when Scary Mary was a he.

Her picture in all its strange made-up glory hit the front page of the newspaper as a primary suspect in the Empty Mummy Murders.

So on the day of the ceremony, Scary Mary could not attend.

I wanted to jump into jail and spring her for the ceremony, but Stan wouldn't let me. He said we didn't do things that way.

I did the best I could in the ceremony, leaving offerings of five thermoses of hot chocolate at each end of the now repaired scar in the land. Silicon Suckers treasured hot chocolate as a sacred drug that allowed them to produce more Silicon Suckers. I figured five at each end would show them how serious I thought the scar was.

Denton, the God of Land Use Planning, who was the God who had originally negotiated the settlement of lands around Las Vegas, appeared and begged for the forgiveness of the great beings.

There just wasn't much else we could do.

No Silicon Suckers showed up, so we left the thermoses sitting in the sand in the desert.

Four days later Scary Mary vanished from her holding cell. Her body was found where the others had been found two days earlier. All her organs had all been cleaned out through her ass and her skin was mummified.

Scary Mary became the fourth known victim of the Empty Mummy Murderer. Of course, the case was never solved.

I was batting zero-for-two. Two women had come to me for help with the Silicon Suckers and both had been killed. I moped around for a few days until finally Patty got fed up with me and went with me to talk with Stan.

We ended up in another floating office far over the city. The view was stunning, but I noticed Stan had his windows turned so that he couldn't see in the direction of the quarry.

He was sitting behind a big oak desk with nothing on it. Patty and I dropped down onto the leather couch.

With Patty pushing me on, I mentioned what was bothering me to Stan.

He just shrugged. "Nothing you could do when a person won't help themselves and just keep their mouth shut."

"I mentioned that a few times as well," Patty said, shaking her head. "But he's determined to feel bad."

"It feels like crap," I said. "Even though I couldn't do anything."

"Yeah, it does," Stan said. "But do you win every hand you play at a poker table?"

"Of course not," I said, almost angry that he had suggested that. "But when I lose a hand there I don't have someone die."

"True," Stan said, "but you win a hell of a lot more than you lose in the saving-people game. And that's the key to remember."

"Yeah," Laverne said, suddenly appearing standing beside Stan behind his desk, "remember the ones you saved."

Patty and I both jumped to our feet, because when Lady Luck appears, you don't sit there slouching on the couch.

Lady Luck went on. "Remember you and your team saved me once. And the entire human race another time. And you've even saved a few people from the Silicon Suckers over the last few years, which is more than most have done."

All I could do was nod. She was right.

"So get over it and get back to work," she said, smiling at me.

When Lady Luck smiles at you, trust me, you can feel it. And I did. I felt a ton better, and was suddenly back thinking again instead of just feeling sorry for myself for losing Scary Mary.

"Stan," Lady Luck said, "teach Poker Boy how to build himself an office, would you? It's about time he and his team have one of their own, don't you think?"

Then she vanished.

Stan laughed and stood from behind his desk. "That's the first time I have ever heard her give a pep talk."

"You're kidding?" I asked, feeling stunned.

"Three thousand years, never seen it happen."

Suddenly even more of the weight seemed to lift from my shoulders.

Patty gave me a hug and then a big, long kiss.

"Hey, not in my office," Stan said.

I broke away from Patty just long enough to say, "Then teach me how to build one of my own." Then I went back to kissing Patty.

"Nag, nag, nag," Stan said.

~

Now Available
from all your favorite booksellers
in trade paper and electronic editions.

Dee W. Schofield

A Story of Too Much Sex.
And Meeting the Perfect Woman.
Just Hope She's Human.

SQUATTER'S RIGHTS

on the Street of Broken Men

Conrad found Tani, the woman of his dreams. Beautiful, sexy, and soft fine hair all over her body that drove him wild.

And Tani found Conrad, exciting, fun, and primitive, something she loved and needed to escape her boring job.

A perfect match? It might have been, except for one minor problem. Tani wasn't from Earth.

Originally written and published under the pen name Dee. W. Schofield.

SQUATTER'S RIGHTS ON THE STREET OF BROKEN MEN
Written under the name Dee W. Schofield

ONE

"FUR," CONRAD WEIR SAID, trying to keep his voice low enough that not every one of the twelve people in the Golden Dragon Bar would hear him in his excitement. "I'm not kidding. She was covered in a fine blonde fur, all over her body. Hottest thing I have ever seen. Or hell, felt."

"Yeah, right," his companion and best friend, John "The Clump" Benson said, staring at his glass of beer on the bar in front of him. "You were so drunk, you just ended up in the zoo screwing one of the bears. Lucky you didn't get your balls chewed off."

A woman in the booth under the fake plants looked over at them and gave them a disgusted look. John's voice could sure carry. But hell, what did she expect being in a local bar like this one? The Dragon, as everyone called this bar, was a place for locals in the afternoons and early evenings, and college kids at night. Conrad was usually gone long before the kids arrived, moving up the street to the Elks Club bar to listen to whatever local band was playing for the week.

The Dragon consisted of five booths against a back wall, a half dozen small tables, and a long bar across the back with ten stools, usually filled with regulars. Dave was the normal afternoon bartender, a quiet kid who had come to town to go to college and had just never left. He could pour a mean drink and listen to just about anything with a straight face. Conrad had no idea what he did outside of the Dragon.

Conrad ignored John's zoo comment and went on, telling him about last night, remembering every detail of the wonderful night with Tani. She had been real, very real, that much he was sure of. He had met her at the Elks when she came in with a group of about six people, one of who must have been a member. He had asked her to dance. At first she had resisted, so he bought her a drink, then another, and after a little talking, he finally got her out onto the dance floor.

That was when he discovered the fine layer of fur all over her skin and he was hooked.

"I couldn't keep my hands off her," he said, letting the memory just flow. "I drove her nuts."

"You drive me nuts," John said, finishing his beer and signaling Dave for another.

"Yeah, but with her, I did it by stroking her arms and legs and stomach and breasts. I couldn't get enough of the fur. Softest, finest hair I have ever felt."

John looked at him like he had lost a bolt and his head was about to fall off. "She had *hair* on her stomach and boobs? Not for me."

Again the woman in the booth snorted and stared into her drink, trying to ignore John's comments as much as she was ignoring the poor guy sitting beside her.

"Fur," Conrad said, making sure his voice didn't carry. "Soft, golden fur, softer than anything you've ever touched. From more than a foot away you can't see it. She has normal skin, wonderful skin, just coated with this fine fur. I loved it. Hell, I think I might be falling in love with her."

"You fall in love with light poles when you're drunk enough," John said. "I've seen it. Remember? I don't think that pole down off of Third Street is ever going to get over you."

Conrad ignored him, even though John was right. Drinking did tend to lower Conrad's restrictions and his judgment. But at the moment, he was cold sober and still felt that way about her. All he could see was her green eyes and wonderful smile. She had a bright wit, a contagious laugh, and oh, *that fur*. A perfect package. What more could any thirty-year-old man want?

"This one might be real," Conrad said, motioning for Dave to bring him something besides the sparkling soda he had first ordered. "Honest."

"Her last name, Einstein?" John asked, looking over at Conrad. "Or maybe a phone number?"

Conrad had to admit he didn't know her last name. Just her first name. Tani. And she had been gone from his apartment like a dream when he woke up this morning. She hadn't even left a note. But that didn't matter. He had met her once, he could find her again. This town wasn't that big.

"That's what I thought," John said when Conrad didn't answer him, again shaking his head and turning back to his beer. He did a lot of that head shaking every time Conrad met a new woman, or had a new idea to make them both rich.

But this time, Conrad was determined to prove him wrong.

"So, you going to help me find her?" Conrad asked his friend as Dave slid his scotch and water, light on the water, onto a napkin and put it in front of Conrad.

"And why would I do that?" John asked. "I helped you find Debbie, remember, and look where that got you."

Debbie had been Conrad's wife, now his ex-wife. John had introduced them at a party up on campus. She had left Conrad for a lawyer and then got remarried and left the state. Good riddance as far as Conrad was concerned. That had been four years ago.

"Friendship," Conrad said, sipping the sharp taste of his drink. He didn't know why he drank scotch, other than to avoid hangovers. The stuff tasted like it could chew the enamel off his teeth. But

after a few drinks, he didn't much notice the taste. But he did notice the lack of headaches and driving the porcelain steering wheel in the morning. Made the taste worthwhile as long as he was going to drink.

John snorted and said nothing about the "friendship" comment.

John and Conrad had been best friends since high school, had gone to college together here. When John had started a construction firm, he had wanted Conrad to join him, but Conrad had instead just worked for him part time. Conrad had ended up going on to more school, getting a graduate degree in math, and then getting hired to teach at the university.

Both of them had been married once and divorced once. They now had a habit of meeting every late afternoon, with a bunch of other locals, in the Dragon for a

drink or two. At thirty, Conrad had never expected to end up divorced, hunting for women in bars, and unhappy in his job after only a few years. But he was.

Tani might change that if he could find her.

John had sworn off women after his divorce, taken up drinking beer and building homes for other people, and was slowly but surely getting a beer gut and very rich.

He had also been a process server while in college and had developed a knack for finding people who didn't want to be found. If anyone could find this Tani, John could.

"So, what do you say?" Conrad asked. He took another sip of the biting taste of scotch, then turned to his best friend.

"You're serious, aren't you?" John asked.

"Very," Conrad said. Again, the image of Tani's green eyes and wonderful smile filled his mind. He wouldn't mind looking into those eyes for a very long time.

John just shook his head, but Conrad knew he had him.

"Tell you what," John finally said after taking another long drink. "You don't find her in the next week, and you still want to find her, I'll help you. But you're on your own for a week."

"Perfect," John said. "For all I know, she might come walking back into the Elks tonight looking for me, or maybe leave a note at my apartment."

"Sure," John said. He finished off his second beer and signaled for another. "But I'd check the zoo. See if one of the sheep is missing from the kids petting area."

Conrad tried to give his friend a serious look. "Not nice. That's the second Mrs. Conrad Weir you're talking about there."

"Baaaaaaa," John said, loud enough to echo clear out into the restaurant.

Conrad laughed, the woman in the booth snorted again, and the night went on.

TWO

TANI-AREAS-FOL-DAN-PEET floated into the Doorways Bar and Fine Dining and let her robot lifts carry her around the tables and to her two friends sitting near a Punk-Tac game. From the looks of it, they had both just arrived a moment or two before her. Neither had a B of C in front of her, and since they had been here every cycle for the past thirty, the robots knew their orders perfectly.

She drifted into her seat and a moment later, all three of their drinks appeared in front of them, freshly made with the exact liquors from any one of a thousand planets. For Tani, her B of C was the Earth drink called a "Screwdriver" made up of a fruit grown on the planet and a real distilled alcohol called "vodka" packed over frozen water cubes. Very strange but very tasty.

Kreble, who loved her drinks sweet, had a B of C from a planet called Diken, where they drank a form of pure sugar, fermented to a degree Tani had not thought possible, then flavored with different types of plant roots.

Too-Tight-Tootie-Two loved her drinks sour, in the same degree that Kreble loved them sweet. Too's B of C had some mixture minerals from a planet with a name no one could pronounce, blended firmly with roots from two of the planet's trees, then mixed with a type of acid.

If Too had too many, her lips turned an ugly black and Tani and Kreble had to lift her back to her place for the night. Tani hated that and she didn't want that to happen tonight. They only had two more days of their vacation on Doorway, before they had to return to their home world, Lind, and return to work.

All three of them worked in an anti-gravity chip plant there, waiting for the right moment to take a mate, have children, and then return to work. Last year Tani had done that twice, spawning her 42nd and 43rd child. She was scheduled for two more matings the coming cycle and two more children.

Boring didn't begin to describe how she felt about that. Especially after last night on Earth with the man who called himself Con-Rad. She was required by custom to produce child 44 and 45 in the coming cycle, but she could pick with whom and Con-Rad might just be a likely mate. It would add to her diversity quota since seldom did anyone mate with creatures from Earth. They were considered far too primitive.

Actually, she wasn't even sure if it was possible, but she would be willing to find out.

But right at this point in her life, Tani needed an adventure, and going into a backwards planet like Earth to mate might be the adventure she needed.

Unlike her two friends, Tani had saved her money and was rich enough to not work. She only did so because she had nothing else to do, and her friends were there. But she had been unhappy with her job for a long, long time. It was time for a change.

And it was this bar that was going to help her make that change, on this vacation.

She looked at her two friends as they took first sips of their drinks, then blurted out, "I'm going back."

"Why would you go back to work two days early?" Too asked, stunned into not drinking for a moment.

"Not back to work," Tani said. "Back to Earth."

"Did you leave something there?" Kreble asked.

"It's that Earther you were doing rubbing with," Tani said.

Tani gave them both her most seductive smile.

"Did you show him your true form?" Kreble said.

"No," Tani said. "I maintained human form. But Earth excites me. Earthers excite me."

"So you're going to use another day of your vacation there?" Too asked. "After we planned on hitting Solo-Prime for their chalk baths and system-clearing tongue-licking?"

"Sounds heavenly," Tani said, not mentioning to her friends they had done the same thing for the last five cycles and once you've had one Solo-Prime insect-tongue clear your system, you've done it more than enough.

"Actually," Tani said. "I'm going to spend the next cycle on Earth exploring the wilderness. I'm going to take a leave from work."

Both her friends just sat staring at her.

Then Too looked like she might get sick. "Seriously, you are considering mating with an Earth creature?"

Tani nodded, sipping the wonderful-tasting screwdriver. "Two of them, actually."

"Is that even possible?" Kreble asked.

Tani just smiled. "I'm sure going to find out."

THREE

AFTER A COUPLE more drinks and then an hour searching through the phone book for any first name that even resembled the name Tani, Conrad gave up and told John that he would buy him dinner if he joined him again at the Elks.

"The Golden Dragon here isn't good enough for you?" John asked.

"Tani can't find me here," John said.

"How can you be so sure?" a woman's voice asked from behind Conrad.

Both men spun on their bar stools, Conrad a little faster than John. He knew that voice anywhere. Even being drunk last night, that voice could soothe even the wildest beast. And excite the hell out of him.

"Tani!" Conrad said, standing and giving her a long hug, which she returned in a wonderful fashion. "I've been looking for you, hoping to see you again."

"You mentioned you liked this place," Tani said, smiling. "So I took a chance."

Conrad almost fainted with that smile. Wow, she was far, far more beautiful than he remembered. And she had done something different with her hair tonight. It was a light brown and looked longer. Clearly the booze last night had done him no good. But right now he was only two scotches into the evening and he planned on doing no more.

Tonight she had on a thin sweater that showed most of her assets and tight slacks that looked more painted on that anything.

"I'm John," he said, extending his hand.

Conrad could tell John was stunned at Tani's beauty as well.

Tani smiled and Conrad thought John's knees might just melt out from under him as he shook her hand.

"Conrad mentioned you," Tani said. "So I brought two friends tonight that you just might find interesting."

Tani turned as two women just as stunning as Tani walked in, looking around at the small bar. Both also had on pants that left nothing to the imagination and tight blouses.

"This is Too," Tani said, introducing the woman with long red hair. "And Kreble."

The woman with short blonde hair shook Conrad's hand, then smiled at John with a smile as powerful as Tani's.

Then Tani looked directly at John and smiled. "Think you can handle my two friends?"

John's mouth opened, then closed, then he just nodded as he swallowed.

Both women giggled as each took one of John's arms and headed for the door.

Tani took Conrad's arm as he stood there, mouth still open, just staring in shock at his best friend. "Let's go with them, find a more private place."

"We can go back to my apartment again," Conrad managed to croak out.

"Perfect," Tani said, stroking his arm as they headed for the door. "My friends want to know if we are compatible. After last night, I'm fairly certain we are. You willing to try that again?"

Flashes of the wonderful night in bed with Tani appeared in Conrad's mind like a movie and he just nodded.

Actually, he just kept nodding all the way to his apartment.

FOUR

SOMEWHERE AROUND six in the morning the squeals and moans from John and the other two women in Conrad's second bedroom stopped.

Conrad was just trying to catch a third or fourth wind. It might be more but the sex and the night had become a long, wonderful blur. Tani didn't seem to be slowing down at all.

"Tani," the woman named Kreble said from Conrad's bedroom door. Conrad was so tired, he didn't even try to cover up the fact that he was nude and sprawled on his back on the bed.

"Yes," Tani said, smiling up at her friend.

"It seems you were right," Kreble said as the other woman appeared beside her. "This species seems to be suitable for mating. And they are fun."

"That they are," Tani said, giving Conrad junior a tug right there in front of her friends.

Conrad just didn't care. Far, far too tired. He hadn't had a night like this ever, let alone at his age.

"Have fun," Kreble said. "We'll see you next cycle."

"If not before," Tani said, smiling.

Then it was if the two other women just vanished. Conrad blinked then started to say something as Tani went back to the job of trying to revive him for another round.

They couldn't have just vanished. He must have dozed off for a micro second.

He reached for Tani to indicate she might want to give him a little more rest, but then his hand found the fine hair on her back and he started stroking it and even to his own surprise, he was soon ready to go again.

John left a few hours later with a smile on his face and an "I owe you, buddy."

Tani didn't leave.

She also didn't know how to cook or even use some basic household appliances like a faucet on the sink or an electric toothbrush. She kept saying that where she was from they didn't have those sorts of things.

But she wouldn't tell Conrad where she was from, other than a name that didn't sound very real. When asked she said her last name was Peet.

But Conrad didn't much care if she was backward and had a weird last name. Tani tended to spend most of her days in the nude and as time went along Conrad stopped drinking, lost weight, and gained stamina that he hadn't even dreamed of as a teenager.

Tani just never quit smiling.

Then one day about a month after Tani moved in she said, "Mating cycle has started. Are you ready?"

She stroked his arm and he touched her fur-covered naked back and he was as ready as he always was.

That was the last night of sex.

On the second day he asked her what happened and she said, "It is forbidden to have sex until the child is born."

She would explain no more, so he left the apartment without her and went back to the Golden Dragon.

"Wow, are you looking good, friend," John said. "Tani getting you in shape, huh?"

Conrad decided to not talk about what had happened with the sudden lack of sex and talk of a kid. So he had two drinks and went home.

Tani was nude, and now clearly pregnant.

He stood staring at her, his mouth open, then just pointed at her stomach. "What is that?"

"Our child," she said, nibbling on a box of chocolates while watching *The Price is Right* rerun.

"When did that happen?" he asked.

She looked at him, puzzled. "Two nights ago, of course. He will be born in two days. My 44th child, but my first with an Earthman. You should be honored."

Conrad just opened his mouth and not a damn word came out. He just couldn't think of anything to say.

He turned around, went back out the door and back to the Golden Dragon. John managed to get him home at closing, but he was so drunk he just stumbled into bed.

The next morning a very, very pregnant Tani awoke him, still nude.

He took a shower, looked at her one more time, then said, "Let me know when this nightmare is over."

He again drank himself into a stupor, took a cab home, and woke up the next morning to the sound of a crying child.

And Tani was back looking like her normal self.

"Would you like to see your son?" she asked, carrying him to the side of the bed for Conrad to see.

The kid looked cute, as most babies do. He had Conrad's slightly thin nose, but like Tani was covered in a fine layer of hair.

How the hell did he have a kid? He had never wanted a kid, and he had only been playing around with Tani for less than a few weeks. Maybe a month at most.

A moment later two strange-looking women with flat faces and black dresses who smelled of mothballs appeared in the bedroom right out of thin air.

"I've got to stop drinking again," Conrad said.

"Say goodbye to your child," Tani said to Conrad.

"What?"

Tani stood and took the child to the two faceless women.

The both held their palms over the child, then nodded. "You risked a great deal, Tani," one of the women said without any sign of a mouth moving anywhere that Conrad could see "to mate with such a primitive creature. But the baby is fine."

Tani nodded and handed them the baby.

A moment later the two faceless women in black and the baby vanished.

Tani turned to Conrad, completely nude. "Now that's finished, let's have some fun."

She jumped on the bed, yanked the covers off him, and sat on his crotch.

"Hold on, hold on," he said, taking her by both arms and keeping her from moving on him. "What just happened?"

"Our duty, of course," Tani said, smiling. "Wonderful isn't it, helping our different races survive and mingle."

She started to move again and his crotch started to respond again, being a traitor, but he needed more information.

"Different races? What do you mean?"

Tani smiled. "I told you, I'm from Lind."

"I have no idea where that's at," he said.

"About a hundred thousand light years from here," she said, still moving on him even though he was holding her two wonderful-feeling arms.

"You're kidding, right?"

"I am not joking," Tani said, smiling at him. "I am very different from you. I am from another planet."

"John put you up to this, didn't he?" Conrad asked.

Tani again smiled. "Would you like to see my actual form?"

"I would love to," he said. "I have no idea what just happened with that baby thing and I need some answers."

She sort of shrugged. "I was warned that you might not be able to understand my original form, which is why I have maintained this body."

"I like this body," he said, stroking the fur on her arms. "But it's always better to know the real person."

Again she shrugged.

And a moment later a huge, fur-covered spider with eight legs, two eyes on stalks, and large green lips with rows of teeth behind them was straddling his naked body.

The last thing he remembered before waking up screaming in the hospital was Tani saying, "Can't say I didn't warn you."

He couldn't stop screaming for a very, very long time.

Two months after being committed to the State Mental Hospital, a small spider crawling down the wall near his bed caused him to have a heart attack and he died at the age of thirty.

FIVE

TANI-AREAS-FOL-DAN-PEET floated into the Doorways Bar and saw her two friends just getting their drinks on this first day of their vacation. It felt wonderful to see them again. She had so much to tell them about her adventure of the cycle.

"How did the mating go with the primitives?" Kreble asked after the ritual greetings were finished.

Tani smiled, her eye-stalks swirling. "They are wonderful playthings and pro-duce adequate children."

"But…" Too said, leaning in and matching one eyestalk with Tani's. "I hear a reservation."

"They ask too many questions," Tani said. "I showed Con-Rad my original form and he ran from me so I had to find another mate for the second child of the cycle."

"Are you going back?" Too asked.

"No," Tani said. "I had wonderful adventures I can share, but I want to keep exploring."

Both of her friends looked and acted relieved. "So where are we going first this vacation?"

"I hear there is a little planet of ocean-swimmers that might be fun."

Both Too and Kreble pretended to be shocked by swirling their eyestalks and twisting their front legs together.

Tani smiled. She knew they were as excited about the idea as she was. Sex with creatures with four sex organs and ten arms under a mile of ocean could promise many, many good times.

She sipped her last Screwdriver from the planet Earth and nodded to her friends. It was good to be home.

Now Available
from all your favorite booksellers
in trade paper and electronic editions.

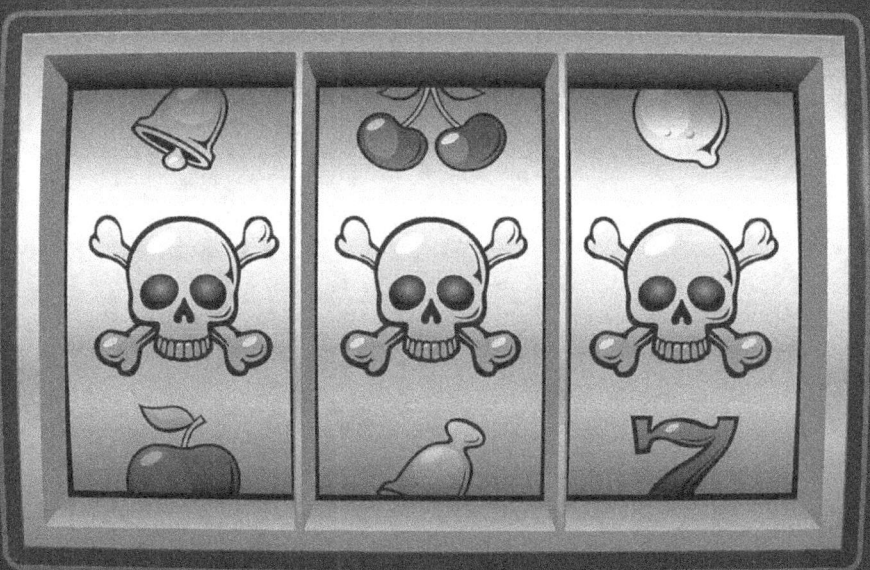

USA Today Bestselling Writer

DEAN WESLEY SMITH

THEY'RE BACK

A Poker Boy Short Novel

In the last of four parts, Poker Boy and his team must confront the worst enemy they ever faced. The dreaded Slots of Saturn once again.

But the Slots of Saturn died years before. How could they be back?

The sequel to the novel The Slots of Saturn, *this short novel appeared first in* Fiction River.

THEY'RE BACK
A Poker Boy Short Novel

Part 4 of 4

CHAPTER SIXTEEN
Planning the Past

PATTY AND I SAT there sipping our vanilla milkshake. It had partially melted while we were on that last visit back into our shared nightmare, but it was still good. And neither of us cared. We were both just trying to get some energy for whatever came next.

The fries were still just warm enough to eat, so we munched on a few of those as well.

I could tell from Patty's hand on mine that she had been drained by helping Sherri and slowing time even more when we were back in time.

Suddenly, across from us, Sherri, who had been sitting, mostly staring at her milk-shake, grabbed her head and bent over in pain.

Screamer instantly had his arm around her and Patty leaned across the table and touched her as well.

I couldn't believe it. The damn slot machines were back again.

I stared at the three of them, wishing I could do something to help.

Stan just sat there staring as well. If a god was helpless, what could I expect to do?

After a moment, Sherri opened her eyes and sat up. Patty leaned back next to me and through the touch in our shoulders I tried to feed her some energy.

"Where are they?" I asked, afraid of the answer.

"A rundown casino out on the old highway," Patty said. "The Golden Jackpot Casino."

"We don't have police on that one," Stan said.

Instantly he and I both jumped to the old casino.

The energy of the evil slot machines pulsed over me like a wave of desire, working to draw me in with the promise of richness and fun, all for a nickel.

An overweight, middle-aged woman, with dyed-brown hair piled far too high for even the 1960s, was headed for the deadly machine. She had on skin-tight green Capri pants that from the back should have had a warning sign attached that told a person to never look. She had a plastic bucket of coins tucked against her left breast and was about five steps from the machine.

Another, even heavier and shorter middle-aged woman dressed in even tighter brown Capri pants was one step behind her.

That was a sight I was never going to get out of my mind, and if it hadn't been for the pulsing Slots of Saturn machines beyond them, I would have turned away.

Stan and I both jumped again, appearing in front of the women.

We acted like security guards, both holding our hands up for them to stop.

Both women did stop, shocked expressions showing through the layers of makeup coating their faces.

Before they could ask where we came from, Stan said. "These machines are broken." His voice echoed through the casino like only a god can make a voice echo.

"They look fine to me," the first woman said, looking past us both. "I love old slot machines."

"Reminds her of her dearly-departed husband," the other woman said, somehow smiling without cracking the layers of makeup.

"He never had a crank like that one," the first woman said, pointing to the long handle with the black nob on the side of the machine.

Both of them laughed.

I shuddered.

"Yeah, you could wish," the second woman said to her friend, and again they laughed.

Behind me I could feel the intense pull of the machines, demanding that someone sit down and feed them.

In front of me were two women who really did belong in the past, but a past far before 2004.

"What can one pull hurt?" the first woman asked, giving Stan a smile that I swore should have broken a couple of layers of caked-on makeup. Her teeth were yellow from too many cigarettes.

"More than you know," Stan said.

He waved his hands at the two women and they vanished.

"Where did you send them?" I asked, looking around to make sure no one had gotten in behind us.

"To the buffet, paid lunch," he said.

"Yeah, that's what they needed," I said, shaking my head.

We spread out a little and for the next three minutes we stood there, backs to the machines, telling people the slots were damaged, as the power of the slots drew people toward them.

Finally, the machines started pulsing bright to dim and then back, more and more, faster and faster, until finally with a flash they jumped back to the warehouse in the past.

They had left empty.

Around us the old casino went on, an occasional bell going off, an occasional yell from a drunk at one of the gaming tables. Without the pulsing energy of the old slot machines, the casino suddenly felt worn and tired. And it smelled of old cigarettes and spilled whiskey on the worn blue carpet.

"Lucky we had Sherri to tell us the slots were here again," I said.

He nodded. "But while you are in the past, she needs to stay here to keep watch."

"I agree," I said.

We both jumped back to my office where Sherri looked like she was just recovering from the jolt of the machine's last jump.

And Patty looked even more tired than before.

I just hoped that at some point this would be over and Patty could rest.

Not that I worried about her or anything.

CHAPTER SEVENTEEN
The Plan

WE KNEW that the other eleven people from the future all came back out of the slot machine in just over an hour period as we rescued everyone. We knew that time exactly.

And we knew who they were and what they looked like, so we could intercept them on the way out of the warehouse to the police that we had stationed outside that first time.

But Hank had arrived in a window that the Bookkeeper could only knock down to four hours.

Four hours to find him and get him back, a couple hours to get everyone else back.

Six hours.

We had eight hours until the time loop locked in and trapped us forever. And not even Kronos, the God of Time, could save us.

That was cutting it very close.

Too close for my tastes.

Laverne appeared and nodded to Stan, then to her daughter, then to me as she sat down. She was now dressed in casual clothes. Jeans and a tan sweatshirt that said, "Believe It" on the front.

"Great job stopping yet another one," she said.

"Sherri knew where it came in," I said. "Stan and I just stood guard."

Laverne nodded. "Good team work. So, who is going back with me to stop this madness?"

I looked around at my team and sighed. I had given this a little thought and I knew I was right. But both Patty and Screamer were not going to like it.

"I think you and Ben and I should go back," I said to Laverne. It felt weird giving Lady Luck instructions, but she had asked after all.

One of her dark eyebrows actually went up at that suggestion, telling me it wasn't what she expected.

Both Screamer and Patty started to object and I held up my hand and they stopped.

"We need to keep Sherri here in case the machines come back. Screamer, you and Patty need to be here to help her through that. In the time we're gone, the slots might come back more than once."

Sherri didn't like the sound of that, but she nodded.

I turned to my boss. "Stan, you need to be here to jump to stop anyone else from getting sent back if the machines do come back again."

Stan nodded.

"That's critical," Laverne said, "because we don't have time to figure all this again."

Screamer nodded and so did Sherri.

I looked at Ben and he smiled.

"Ben knows exactly what each person looks like," I said, "so we're not trusting my memory completely. And he knows which casino they came from in this time, and when, so they can be transported to that same spot close to the time they left. That way they will never be reported missing."

Lady Luck smiled, but Patty didn't look happy.

"I'll work with my friend Johnny in the past," I said. "He was the local cop friend that helped us. He can help me pull out the right ones and keep them from going outside to the police. We'll jump them out from back in the shadows of the warehouse."

And then I looked at Lady Luck. "And you get to do all the transporting through time to where Ben says they need to go."

"A sound plan," Laverne said. "We need to get going, we're cutting this a little close."

I turned to Patty and kissed her.

She kissed me back, then said, "Make this work."

"I'll do my best," I said, smiling at her. Then as I pulled away I said, "Just have the raspberry soap ready to go."

"Oh, damn you two," Screamer said.

Sherri blushed and Patty blushed and Ben just shook his head.

It made me smile.

A moment later, Lady Luck transported me and Ben and herself ten years into the past and into the middle of a dark warehouse full of old and creepy slot machines stacked in rows that seemed to go on forever.

All of them dead, looking very much like tombstones in a graveyard in the dim light.

To one side of the warehouse was a very dangerous set of slots pulsing, sending off a light that made the big warehouse seem even more daunting and huge.

And then with a bright flash, the warehouse went completely dark.

"They jumped," I said.

"And as soon as they come back," Ben said in the dark, "we'll know if we are in the right time window."

"I hope so," Lady Luck said, her voice beside me in the dark. "We have very little margin of error."

CHAPTER EIGHTEEN
Finding Hank

WHILE THE MACHINES were gone I teleported to the front of the warehouse where I remembered a light switch being, and flipped it on.

Overhead lights clicked on, showing the gigantic size of this slot graveyard. It had to be at least two football fields long and another one wide, and the slots were stacked on shelves a good twenty feet over my head in long rows from front to back.

Laverne and Ben joined me and we went over to one side at the head of the aisle where the slots were. I pointed to a tarp that still seemed to be covering something, only if you looked hard, there was nothing there. The tarp just seemed to be floating in space. Some part of the machine never left the warehouse when it jumped.

"My gut sense is that riding on the outside of this thing isn't going to be a pleasant experience," I said. "Hank will appear under that tarp, more than likely knocked out cold."

Both Laverne and Ben nodded.

"I'm going to check the other doors to make sure none of them are unlocked or broken open from the inside," I said. "I know he didn't go out the front door because it had a padlock on it when we arrived the first time."

"Good thinking," Ben said.

I teleported to the back of the warehouse and checked the door on the right. Secure. I jumped to the garage door and it was also secure.

Suddenly I heard Laverne in my head, *They are returning.*

I jumped back to where they were just as the machine appeared under the tarp.

There was no one in the chair under the tarp.

Damn.

The machines sat there, covered, their glow taunting me, pulling me to go sit down at them.

"Wow, that's some pull," Ben said.

"They are very powerful," Laverne said.

"I'm going to check the other door," I said.

I jumped and the instant I saw the door, I knew we were in trouble. It had been broken out from the inside.

Hank had already gotten out into the world.

I jumped back to Laverne and Ben. "He's been here," I said.

"Damn," Lady Luck said. "When was the previous jump that we know about?"

"Six hours ago," Ben said.

Laverne nodded and looked up. "Kronos, help?"

Suddenly we were back in a dark warehouse, and again through the darkness, the machine was pulsing, getting ready to jump.

"Check the door," Laverne said a moment before I vanished to do just that.

It was locked and hadn't been broken out.

"Thank the heavens," I said.

I flipped on the lights from near the back door and was about to jump back to Laverne and Ben when suddenly Hank appeared out of nowhere and hit me on the side of the head.

I had a fraction of an instant of warning from one of my superpower senses, but they were tuned to slower warnings like what I needed at a poker table.

Not someone about to hit me.

But still I managed to move just enough to cause Hank's intended blow with an old slot handle to just graze my head.

I went down hard, but somehow stayed alert enough to say, "Hank's here!"

And then I took myself out of time, freezing Hank as he was about to smash open the back door of the warehouse.

Ben and Laverne appeared above me in the time bubble.

Ben reached down and helped me to my feet.

"You all right?" Laverne asked, frowning and looking at the side of my head like a worried mom.

I could feel I was bleeding slightly from a gash on the side of my head, and I knew for a fact I was going to have a nasty headache, but I wasn't about to tell Lady Luck herself that I wasn't all right.

"I'll be fine," I said. "My Spidey sense warned me just in time."

Ben laughed.

Laverne just looked puzzled.

"I'm going to take him back," Laverne said, nodding at Hank.

She waved a hand at him and he went to the ground like a sack of very rotten Idaho potatoes.

"Wow, nifty power," I said. "Can I learn that one?"

She laughed. "Hang around for a few more centuries and I might teach it to you. I'll tell everyone at the office we got Hank and then be back."

Then she and Hank were gone.

Ben handed me a wad of Kleenex from his pocket for the bleeding and I nodded thanks. I pressed it against the side of my head as we started walking silently up the aisle between shelves and shelves of old slot machines, a reminder of many people's dead dreams.

CHAPTER NINETEEN
Johnny Does a Double Take

LAVERNE APPEARED as we neared the front.

"They stopped another attack," she said. "And they were happy we got Hank."

I nodded. Damn I missed Patty, even being away from her for this long seemed wrong these days. We were a team. I was stronger and smarter and much calmer with her around.

"I'm going to jump us to about a half hour before you guys start bringing people out," Laverne said.

"Too close," I said. "It took us a while to figure it out. Make it forty-five minutes."

She nodded and the next thing I knew we were standing off on the other side of the warehouse, away from the Slots of Saturn.

Something really bothered me and I looked around. Then as I heard the doorknob rattle, I knew the problem.

"Lights."

I teleported to right in front of the front door, clicked off the lights, and jumped back to a spot beside Laverne.

A moment later I heard my own voice and the lights came back on.

"Quick thinking," Ben whispered.

We stood there for the next half hour, listening to the echoes of our talk, letting me relive once again one of the most horrid times of my life. But now from what seemed like the grandstands.

If I didn't already have a headache from the hit across the head, this time-travel stuff would give me one.

Then, finally, my younger self and Patty and Screamer started rescuing people from the machine.

"Here we go," I whispered. "Ben, you watch and when you see the first one, you tell Laverne."

He nodded.

"Do you need to be touching the person to jump them back to our time?"

"No," Lady Luck said. "Ben just tell me when and where as exact as you can."

"I will," he said.

We stood in the shadows, watching as Johnny and Geneva helped the rescues from the Slots of Saturn out into the hot air and the waiting arms of ambulances and police.

"The first one," Ben said, nodding as Johnny brought her around the corner from the machines and started toward the front door, helping her along as he went.

He then told Lady Luck exactly when, right to the minute, and which casino the woman had come from and what area.

Laverne nodded. "Be right back."

The woman disappeared right out of Johnny's arms.

I stepped forward and motioned for Johnny to come into the shadows with me.

"Poker Boy?" he asked, looking very puzzled and looking back over his shoulder at the same time.

"It's me," I said.

"Geneva says you are still back there getting another person out."

"I am," I said. "That me, from this time. I'm from ten years in the future."

He started to open his mouth and I waved my hand. "We have some people the machine took from my time ten years in the future. We will just be taking those people out of your hands and getting them back to where they belong. But you and Geneva keep this to yourselves. Don't ever tell the other me, or anyone for that matter. Okay?"

He nodded, still looking puzzled and hesitant.

"Go back to work," I said. "It is critical you and the team over there get the people out of that machine."

He nodded and turned away.

I teleported back into the shadows in another aisle so when he looked back, I would have vanished.

Laverne appeared and nodded she had been successful. But she was looking a little tired.

And that bothered me a lot.

I glanced at Ben and he was looking at her as well, looking worried.

Lady Luck should never look tired.

Ever.

CHAPTER TWENTY
A Change of Plans

AFTER THE NEXT two jumps for Laverne back to the present, she looked horrible.

When she came back after the second one, she actually staggered some.

I looked at Ben and he looked very concerned.

I needed to do something and do it fast.

"Change of plans," I said as we waited for the next one from the future. "We have eight more and we're going to hold them all here and all of us jump as a group back to my office. Can you do that?" I asked Laverne. "Just one more jump?"

"I think so," she said, her voice weak. "Kronos warned me this might not be possible. Time jumping takes a massive amount of energy. More than I had imagined, actually. More than I have ever spent in thousands and thousands of years."

That was not something I wanted to hear.

"Just sit there against those slots in the shadows and rest," I said. "Ben and I will get the other eight people rounded up."

She nodded and slid down to the ground. "Thanks."

I looked at Ben and he nodded and we went back to watching the people being rescued from the machine. In all my years, I would never have imagined giving Lady Luck orders, let alone seeing one of the most powerful gods in all the universe exhausted.

Now I just hoped she had enough energy to get us all back at once to my office. From there, Stan could take care of getting the survivors to the right places and times. Otherwise, all of us were going to be stuck in a very ugly time loop that ended with Patty and me ten years apart.

I didn't even want to think about that.

"Next one," Ben said.

The woman was being escorted by Johnny.

I stepped out into the light and walked up to Johnny, who again looked surprised to see me.

"That's one of them," I said. "We need her to wait in here with us."

Johnny nodded and I led the way into a side aisle. I quickly pulled a few tarps off of slots and put them on the concrete. "Just sit there and rest," I said to the woman. "We'll have you home shortly."

"Another one," Ben said as Geneva escorted another man from our time toward the front door.

I moved out as Johnny headed back toward the machines and motioned for Geneva to bring the man over and I had him sit on the tarp as well.

"What's going on?" he demanded.

"We're trying to get you home," I said.

He started to stand and I froze him, pulling myself and Ben out of time.

"We need help," I whispered to Ben.

He nodded. "Who can we trust?"

I knew at once who to call.

"Stan," I said, "A little help?"

Ben shook his head. "Stan can't jump through time."

"I can't what?" Stan asked, then looked at me and Ben.

"Oh," Ben said.

I had called the Stan of this time, not the future Stan.

"That you, Ben?" Stan asked, smiling. "What are you doing here? It's been a long time."

"Working on Poker Boy's team from ten years in the future," Ben said.

Stan started to open his mouth and I stopped him. "We can't tell you anything and you can't say a word that you saw us here."

"What's happening?"

"We're trying to rescue people the machine took from ten years in the future," I said.

His face went white as he instantly understood some of the problem.

"We need help with holding these people in place until the last ones get out of the machine and we can jump them all back to the future."

He nodded.

"Can you help us and never say a word, not even to Laverne."

"Does she know you are here?" he asked.

"I do," Laverne said, staggering around the corner and again sitting down, her back against a slot machine. "But I'm blocking my past self or any other gods from seeing any of this."

Stan nodded. "Not a word. What can I do?"

"Hold these people while Poker Boy and Ben round up the rest," Laverne said. "Then give me an energy boost when I try to jump us all back to our time."

"I can do that," he said, nodding.

I dropped the time bubble and Ben turned back to the steady stream of people again starting from the machines toward the front door.

Behind me the two people from the future were sitting on the floor, frozen, not moving.

Another power I really needed to learn at some point.

CHAPTER TWENTY-ONE
Too Close—Far, Far Too Close

After we had the seventh person sitting frozen on the tarp, I looked at Ben. "How much time do we have?"

"Thirty-seven minutes," he said. "The last one from the future should be out in fifteen minutes."

"Well," I said, "that's going to be a long fifteen minutes."

He only nodded.

"And this is cutting it far, far too close."

Again he nodded.

"Too close?" Stan asked.

"You'll know in ten years. If this works."

I looked at Lady Luck. She was still sitting on the floor with her eyes closed. But at least now she had some color in her cheeks again, as much as I could see color in the gray shadows of the thousands of dead slot machines towering around us.

Stan just kept staring at me, shaking his head.

"Sorry, can't tell you anything," I said, smiling at him. "You know that."

He laughed. "Hell, this is going to be a tough enough secret to hold for ten years."

"Well, keep it," I said, "and we'll all owe you big time."

"That we will," Lady Luck said, without opening her eyes.

After that, we stood there, watching each and every person rescued from the Slots of Saturn be helped to the front door of the warehouse and out into the heat of the day.

I forced myself to relax as much as possible. I had a hunch that Ben and I both were going to have to help Laverne make this jump to the future. I wasn't sure how, but I bet it would include feeding her energy. Last thing we would need would be to get stuck five years from now.

Finally, after what seemed like an eternity as time had slowed down and slowed down, Ben said, "That's him."

I also recognized the guy being escorted by Johnny.

I moved out into the light and took the dazed man's arm, then looked at Johnny. "This is the last one. Remember, not a word."

"You got it."

"Thanks," I said.

"I expect when the timelines catch up, you find me with a full explanation."

"I promise," I said.

I took the man over into the shadows where Laverne was now standing.

"Gather everyone together tightly," she said.

Her voice still didn't sound strong, but it sounded better than it had a little bit ago.

Stan and I and Ben did what she asked, with the eight people from the slot all in some sort of trance. I have no idea how Stan did that, but I sure wanted to know.

I'd ask him if this worked and we got back.

"Push them tight together," Laverne said. "The three of us need to be holding hands around them.

Stan helped us arrange that until I was pushed in tight against a middle-aged woman wearing far too much perfume. I just hoped I didn't sneeze in the middle of all this.

I had a hold of Laverne's hand on one side and Ben's on the other.

"Stan, stay about five feet away," Laverne said, "but focus as much energy at me as you can right now."

I could feel the energy pouring from Stan into Laverne as Stan stepped back and leaned forward and focused at Laverne.

Then, after a few moments of soaking in energy from Stan, Laverne said, "Ben, Poker Boy, on the count of three, focus every bit of energy you both have through your hands to me."

"Understood," I said, taking a deep breath.

"Understood," Ben said.

"Kronos," Lady Luck said into the air. "A little help would be appreciated right about now."

Then with Stan still focusing energy at her, Lady Luck said, "One. Two. Three. Go!"

Every ounce of energy I had I imagined it pouring through my fingers and into Lady Luck. I knew how to do that since Patty and I did that all the time with each other, but not at this level.

I felt like I was turning myself inside out.

This was life or death.

There was no point in holding back any ounce of energy if I ever wanted to see Patty again.

And that thought made me pour out even more energy to Lady Luck.

Around us the warehouse vanished.

And then nothing for the longest time, or what seemed to be the longest time.

I just kept pushing energy at Laverne with all my focus.

Suddenly, we were in my office floating over the city of Las Vegas, in front of the big booth.

The eight survivors and Laverne and Ben and I all tumbled to the ground in a bad imitation of a mass Twister Game gone horribly wrong.

The woman with too much perfume smashed me into the floor.

The only thing I remember seeing was Patty's wonderful face, panicked as she jumped out of the booth to come and help.

Then the room went black as I think I passed out.

CHAPTER TWENTY-TWO
The Magic Touch

I wasn't sure how long it was, but the next thing I remember was Patty stroking my forehead lightly. I could feel a little energy from her touch reviving me a little.

Every bone in my body ached.

And my head hurt from where Hank had hit me with that slot machine handle.

And I wanted to sneeze something awful.

I opened my eyes and smiled at the love of my life, who was smiling at me with those huge brown eyes of hers.

"You all right?"

"No idea," I said, honestly.

She helped me sit up.

I was still on the floor in front of the booth and Madge was hurrying in with three glasses of water.

Sherri and Screamer were sitting next to Laverne on the floor and Stan was helping Ben to sit up.

"What happened to all the people?" I managed to ask with a hoarse throat.

Patty handed me a glass of water that tasted wonderful and gave me even more energy.

"Kronos brought Burt and some of the other gods and got them all back to their right places and times," Stan said.

Laverne nodded. Then she looked at Stan with a look that I hoped someday to have her look at me with. "Thank you."

"Yes, thank you," I said, smiling at my boss.

He smiled. "It was worse in the last five hours knowing what I knew from that side, but not knowing how we got there, or if it would even work. Kronos says it did. We're back in the main time-line. Everything is reset."

Patty hugged me, smiling, and I could feel even more energy pouring through me.

"Mom," Sherri said, "Let me get you home and into bed."

Lady Luck nodded, but didn't move. "Stan, want to jump us both there and come back. Not sure if I dare risk it yet."

Stan nodded and the three of them vanished.

Patty was working to get me to my feet and into the booth and Screamer was helping Ben up from the floor when Stan appeared.

"Stan, same kind of help if you don't mind?" Ben asked.

Stan nodded and smiled. He looked at me. "We have some talking to do."

"Tomorrow," I said.

He laughed. "Tomorrow. Great work, once again."

He vanished with Ben.

"You two going to be all right?" Screamer asked.

I nodded. "After some rest."

"Great work," he said, "as always."

"You too," I said. "Tell Madge we're done for the night."

He nodded and turned and went through the door into Madge's Diner.

Outside the windows of my office, I could see the hint of sunrise starting to color the eastern hills. Below, the lights of Vegas looked wonderful.

It felt great to be home.

I couldn't remember being so tired.

And so satisfied at the same time. Especially sitting there in the booth of my office, holding Patty.

Finally, she pushed away from me and waved her hand. "You need a shower, big boy."

"Sweat?" I asked, smiling at her.

"Perfume," she said.

I stood and she held me as we headed for the door to her apartment below.

"You might need to soap me up some," I said, smiling at her. "I'm pretty tired."

"Raspberry soap?" she asked, smiling back and hugging me.

"Of course," I said. "Just like the first time ten years ago."

"I don't think either one of us has the energy to do what we did that first time ten years ago," she said, kissing me as we went through the door and into her wonderful apartment.

And, of course, she was right.

But the next night we certainly tried to repeat what we had done ten years before in that wonderful shower with that wonderful-smelling soap.

And we honestly came pretty darned close.

And in sex and raspberry soap showers, pretty darned close is pretty darned nice.

~

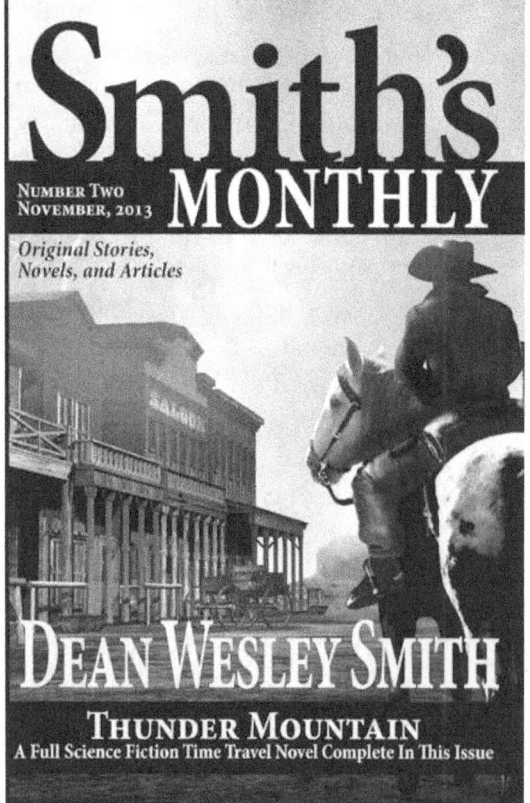

Now Available
from all your favorite booksellers
in trade paper and electronic editions.

Dean
Wesley Smith

USA Today
Bestselling Writer

A LIFE IN
WHOOPEES

Great Moments Exist For All of Us

Great moments exist for all of us at different times in our lives. From a simple taste of a cookie to meeting the love of our life.

Bill Wallace lived through five of those special moments. Bill considers himself lucky to experience five. Many people never get any.

USA Today bestselling writer Dean Wesley Smith peeks inside Bill Wallace's life and his special moments.

A LIFE IN WHOOPEES

My name is Bill Wallace, I'm seventy-two years old, and I feel like one of the lucky people in life. I had a good marriage, great children and grandchildren, a good career. And I had five whoopee moments.

I hear some people never even have one.

My First Whoop

I WAS TEN. It was the last day of school before Christmas, and it was snowing lightly outside our family house in Madison, Wisconsin. As I came through the door, the warmth of the house hit me in the face, combined with the fantastic smell of Mom baking Christmas cookies.

"Yes!" I shouted. I dropped my backpack on the hall table and headed toward the kitchen.

"Billy!" my mom shouted from the kitchen. "Take off your boots at the door."

I stopped, yanked off my boots and went sliding in my stocking feet on the hardwood floors to get a cookie.

That Christmas turned out to be the best Christmas ever, since Grandma and Grandpa were there, Dad was still living at home, and Mom seemed happy. None of that would ever happen again, so I still look back at that Christmas as the best ever.

My Second Whoop

DEBBIE PUSHED me away and slid back across the front seat of the car. She was clearly breathing hard and as excited as I was.

We had parked on a canal road a good four miles outside of town. The only thing close was a farmer's house a half mile away. I still had the car radio on, and the light from it and the moon through the steamed-up windows was enough for me to see Debbie's face.

Her short brown hair was messed up slightly, and her cheeks were red.

Debbie and I were both sophomores in high school and had been sort of hanging out for a month or so together. It was common knowledge that we were together, and we went out on sort-of dates a lot, but that was about as far as it had gotten.

Twice after I had gotten my driver's license, we had parked out here on the canal bank, and both times all we had done was kissed. I was hoping tonight might be a little different, but so far it was turning out to be the same.

The seat between us was one of those bench seats that only Dodges and pick-up trucks had during the seventies. Luckily my mom had bought a Dodge.

"Billy, you promise you won't tell anyone we're parking?"

"Who am I going to tell?" I asked. "Of course I promise. What happens here, what we talk about here, is just between you and me."

She looked at me for a long time, but of course, in that situation, any amount of time seemed long. Then, in a quick motion, she slipped her sweater over her head and tossed it into the back seat.

Her white bra was like a beacon in the night. All I could say was "Wow!"

Five years later, during our second years in college, we were married. I have to admit that even after we were married the sight of her in a bra still took my breath away.

My Third Whoop

THE LETTER came from the State Bar association. Four years of college and three years of law school and it all came down to one stupid envelope in my hand.

I just stood there in the doorway of our apartment, staring at the envelope. I couldn't stop my hand from shaking.

Debbie, who had spent seven years putting me through college, looked at what I was holding, then gently took it out of my hand.

I was already an associate at *David, David, and Jennings*, one of the best law firms in town. But I still had to pass the bar, and the results of that bar exam were inside the envelope. Three weeks ago I had walked out of the exam convinced I had passed, but with every day since I became less and less sure, to the point where I could hardly sleep I was worrying about it so much.

I couldn't watch as Debbie quickly opened the letter.

Then, in the loudest release of breath I had ever heard, she handed me the letter and then hugged me, smiling and crying at the same time.

I glanced at the letter. I had passed.

"Oh, thank God!" I said.

"You did it," Debbie said.

I looked her right in the eye and shook my head. "We did it."

All both of us could do after that was just smile.

My Fourth Whoop

MY SECRETARY knew what I liked. We'd been having an affair for almost a year, and she said that she had something very special for me for Christmas this year.

Debbie and I had had two kids, a boy named Ben and a daughter named Karen. With Debbie focusing on the kids and me focusing on building my law practice, we sort of drifted apart. At some point a few years back we just sort of stopped making love, one or the other of us seeming to always be too busy. We talked about it once in a while, but never really acted on the talk.

We also fought a lot, especially right after the kids were born. It seemed I never knew when I went home if Debbie was going to be angry or not.

I don't think Debbie knew I was having an affair with my secretary, Heather, and I never wanted her to find out. She had developed a real temper over the years, and I sure didn't want her letting that temper loose on me for something as major as an affair. It was bad enough on the small stuff with the kids and the house and money.

Heather knew I was never going to leave Debbie, and she didn't much care. She was open sexually and had no thoughts at all of wanting me as a husband.

"So what's this surprise you've been talking about?" I asked Heather as I came back into my office after my last meeting. It was a little after six in the evening three days before Christmas, and Debbie didn't expect me home for at least another few hours.

Heather beamed at me, her twenty-something smile lighting up the room. She had long blonde hair, even longer legs, and a body that looked far too good in a lace bra and underwear.

"This way," she said, motioning me with a finger.

She had that sexy look on her face and I knew I was in for something fun.

She led me into my darkened office, and then before I could turn on the light, she put her hand on mine and said, "Not yet. I'll tell you when."

She closed the door and turned the lock, sending the room into almost complete blackness, since the blinds were down on the window and it was a dark night outside.

I could hear a faint rustling in the dark. Then Heather said, "Go ahead."

I snapped on the light. The sight that greeted me was something I could have only dreamed about. Heather and another young woman were both sitting on the edge of my desk. Both were wearing only lace underwear. The sight took my breath away, so it was a moment before I finally said, "Wow!"

Heather smiled at me. "This is Heidi, a friend of mine. She's going to help me give you a very special Christmas present."

Two and a half hours later I finally managed to stagger to my car. Never, in all my life, had a Christmas been like this one.

My Fifth and Final Whoop

I WAS just over an hour late getting home after my special present from Heidi and her friend. I expected to find Debbie sitting in her favorite chair, watching television, wrapped in her blue bathrobe, more than likely angry at me. But instead, when I opened the door, I was greeted with the wonderful smell of baking cookies.

I took off my coat and dropped my briefcase on the hall table, then headed for the kitchen. I had skipped dinner because of Heather's little surprise, so the smell of the cookies was almost more than my rumbling stomach could handle.

When I went through the kitchen door, I got a sight that not in a million years would I have expected to see. Debbie was leaning over the stove in her white lace bra and underwear, taking out a fresh batch of cookies.

Until that moment I hadn't realized just how attractive she still was. Even after having two children, she had kept herself fit.

"Wow!" I said, for the second time in the same night.

She looked up at me and smiled. "Welcome home. I thought I'd give you a little surprise."

I glanced around, then back at her. "Where are the kids?"

"At my mother's for the night," Debbie said, smiling her old sexy smile. "So we're all alone."

She put the hot batch of cookies on the stovetop, closed the oven, and moved over to a plate of cookies already frosted. "I bet you're hungry," she said, offering the plate to me.

"I am," I said, taking two cookies. "And these smell wonderful. And you look wonderful."

I almost swallowed the first cookie whole, it tasted so good.

"I do, don't I?" she asked, turning around so that I could see her from all sides.

"You do," I agreed between bites of the second cookie. "Really good."

"As good as Heather and her friend Heidi?"

I froze in mid-bite, staring at her smile.

She laughed, twirling around to give me another look. "I'm surprised you would even be interested after what those two young things put you through in your office."

I had no idea what was happening, how she knew about Heather and what had happened in my office, or how she was even going to react. So being a good attorney and a fearful husband, I ventured nothing, and said nothing.

She leaned against the counter across the kitchen from me, that damned white lace bra of hers making her look very sexy. "Surprised, huh?"

I nodded slightly and she laughed.

It was getting damned hot in that kitchen at that moment. Too hot.

"Didn't you know I would find out what you were doing? Hell, I went to take you to dinner to talk about things and even got a little show tonight."

Damn, she had a key to my office. I had made her one years ago.

"So I thought I'd just come home and give you a little show of my own."

I could feel my heart racing, my blood pounding through my head. I couldn't seem to think straight.

I tried to say something, but the words didn't want to come out.

"Oh, good," Debbie said, laughing and coming toward me, "the poison is working."

I wanted to say, "Cookies?" but again nothing came out.

The next instant, instead of staring at Debbie's white bra, I was watching the tile Debbie and I had picked out specially for the kitchen come rushing up at my face.

I woke up six hours later in the hospital. A woman who looked like a doctor was standing over me, frowning.

"Poison," I managed to croak out.

"We know," she said, nodding and staring at some instrument beside me. Then she patted my arm. "Just rest."

I must have rested, because the next thing I remembered was waking up to the blinding light from the window, my head pounding so hard I thought it might explode.

Debbie was already in jail. She served a total of six years in prison for trying to kill me.

I lost my position in the firm and had to hang out my own shingle because it came out in court what Heather and I were doing that caused Debbie to snap.

The kids lived with me, with my parents helping out, and visited their mother every other Sunday while she was in jail, and every other week after she got out and got a job. I never did make as much money as I had been making at the firm, but I did all right for myself over the years. And never once hired a secretary.

I never remarried either. Couldn't see much point in it.

I was thirty-two when Debbie poisoned me with that cookie. Now I'm seventy-two, no longer practice law, and have three wonderful grandkids. But in all those years, I never had another whoopee moment.

I guess I should be happy to have a five-whoopee life.

From what I understand, some people never even have one.

I feel sad for them.

Dean
Wesley Smith
USA Today Bestselling Writer

When You Just
Don't Have the Time
to Wash the Green Rambler

BETWEEN SHOWERS

All he wanted to do was wash his green Rambler Classic, but the volcano blew and started dumping ash everywhere.

And just wouldn't stop.

An end-of-the-world story for one man who just really wanted it to rain.

And yes, I lived downwind from Mount St. Helens in 1980, and that is where this story came from.

BETWEEN SHOWERS

ONE

IT RAINED YESTERDAY, which was the day before the volcano blew.

I was annoyed at the rain, because it caught me by surprise. Actually, I was napping at the time, but I was still surprised when I woke up. Not a fun-surprise sort-of-thing, either.

The rain, in its untimely arrival, had given me no time to get my freshly-washed-and-waxed green Rambler Classic under the shelter of the overhang on the back of my house. I usually wash my car three times a week, and when I saw, to my surprise, that it had rained, I figured I was going to have to wash it again today. In fact, I prepared myself last evening for a morning of car washing.

But that was before the volcano blew.

Everything changes when volcanoes blow.

Now, as ash drifts down outside my living room like a lazy snow, covering every-thing in a gray blanket, growing deeper by the hour, I hope for rain.

Rain, I believe, would clean out the air, turn the ash into mud, and make it safe.

One day I am mad at the rain, the next I hope for it. I am clearly divided in my rain loyalties.

I am also a divided surprise junkie, it seems. Yesterday, I was angry at the surprise of the rain, now I want to be surprised again by it. I have even thought of napping to see if the rain would come. But after tossing and turning on the couch for a half hour I came to the conclusion that sleeping just after a volcano blows is not possible for me. It might be for some people, but not for me.

So maybe my inability to sleep will hold off the rain.

I feel powerless without the ability to nap. I can only now hope for rain, wish for rain, think about rain.

I thought for a short time about praying for rain, but on that strategy I have a problem. I am not a religious man. Religion hasn't come to me in a flash of lightning, or even an itch like a bad fungus between my toes. I haven't caught it like a cold, or ran into it like a car wreck. It just hasn't happened to me, so I can't pray for rain. No god to pray to.

Just hoping and wishing and thinking are my choices, and I alternate between those choices as the ash builds up outside.

TWO

LOOKING THROUGH my front window feels like viewing the world through an old black-and-white television.

I had bought an old black-and-white television a number of years back from a thrift shop. It had a big wood cabinet with carved legs and round marks on the top where people had left glasses and scarred the wood. It only worked for a day and then smoke came out of the back. I now use it for a stand to hold up the smaller color television with no circle stain marks that I bought six months later from the same thrift shop.

Right now that color television is working just fine, only there is no picture. Just gray fuzz like the ash outside.

I walk back and forth in my living room, first staring out the window, then going back to stare at the empty television. The gray in the television and the gray in the windows is turning my entire life gray, sucking the colors from my green living room carpet, my old maroon reading chair, even the covers of my books stacked in the corners.

Everything is becoming the color of a road surface, bland and without contrast.

I love contrast in things. A day without contrast just isn't a good day for me. Today is not a good day. It needs to rain to change that. The wet of the rain needs to contrast with the dry of the ash. That would make it a good day.

I stare at the television again. The man who did the nightly news had looked alarmed when he had come on and said to stay tuned for further emergency messages, but that had been a half hour ago.

I figure it was lucky, at least so far, that the power hadn't gone out. If it does, I am prepared, with candles and matches and everything, even though it is still sort of light outside.

Actually, it is just a little after two in the afternoon, but the cloud of ash falling from the sky has turned the day into dusk.

I stop and put my face against the window like a kid staring into a candy store. Outside the ash is halfway up the post on my slightly-tipped mail box that sits just off the edge of my driveway.

I have been meaning to straighten the post because I hate to leave a message to the world that I thought the mail was a crooked thing. Actually, I have no opinion of the mail system in this country. I have just never got around to fixing the mailbox post.

Getting around to things often is my worst problem, or at least that was what my mother used to say.

The one girlfriend I had had since I got out of school had said the same thing. It seemed I didn't get around to her often enough either. I would have, if she hadn't slammed the door in my face and left.

I stare out the window again as I pace. The ash looks light and fluffy and fun to walk through. It might be. At one point I thought about going outside to test the theory, but then the emergency folks warned over the television that everyone should stay inside because the ash might be poisonous.

That warning had made me look at the gray stuff completely differently, shifting my perspective from fun and light to gray and dangerous. Amazing how a simple warning can change perspectives of a person like that.

Poison gray snow is falling from the sky. That is worse than yellow snow I figure. Yellow or gray, either way I am going to do what the man on the news channel had said to do, and stay inside.

The power flickers.

I hold my breath as if holding my breath will help the power stay on.

Maybe it did, because the power stabilizes again, leaving the television still showing gray, and the window still showing gray.

I go back to hoping and wishing and thinking about rain, which is better than thinking about the power going out.

Before my phone had stopped working, I had talked to my old buddy Mike about the ash coming our way. That had been just after the volcano blew this morning, and the first warnings about a heavy ash fall to the west of the volcano were being sent out.

That was also before the big gray cloud rolled in from the east. It had been a sunny day. Perfect car-washing weather. And the man on the radio had said as I was waking up that there was no chance of rain for the next few days.

Mike had said that rain would eventually wet down the ash and turn it into mud, and that we were all going to be stuck in our houses until the next rain.

After seeing the ash reach halfway up the mail box post, I am starting to believe him, even though I hadn't when he said it.

Now I hope for rain, and wait for the man on the television to come back on to tell me what to do.

And I pace.

Pacing is something to do. I take turns staring at the gray television and the gray world outside the window, and pacing between the two.

But pacing doesn't seem like enough. There has to be something I can do.

Then the thought comes to me: Maybe I can bring rain.

I dig through a pile of books behind my reading chair and find an old Native American rituals book. Actually, the title is *Indian Rituals and their Practice*. The book had been published at least fifty years before the turn of the last century. I still make myself think of the book as the Native American rituals book, and never look at the real title.

In chapter six the author talks about the different types of rain dances. I stare at the old black and white pictures. I could look the part of a Native American. I could get a few feathers left over from an old Halloween turkey decoration I had in the attic, then stick the feathers in the headband I use for jogging.

I think about the idea for a moment. I could also use some lipstick left behind by my old girlfriend as ceremonial paint on my forehead. She had used it for ceremonial occasions on her lips, so I figure it would work fine.

I could be a real rain dancer.

Then I realize I don't know the steps. I had never been a good dancer, and more often than not girls in school had laughed at my attempts. It is bad enough having high school girls laugh at you. Having the rain laugh would be another matter. Much worse I am sure.

And there is no Rain Dancing school that I can attend to learn in enough time to make a difference.

I put the book behind my reading chair and go back to pacing and watching the different versions of the same show. Gray world through the window, gray television on the air.

On the television nothing happens, outside the window the ash has now reached the top of the mailbox.

Suddenly the television blares out an alarm, reminding me that I had kept the sound up earlier when I had gone into the bathroom, just in case it had come back. If I had been in the bathroom and that alarm sounded, I would have heard it just fine. Standing beside the television, it gives me a very sharp surprise.

And not a rain surprise.

I turn the sound down to normal levels just as a man's face replaces the sign that reads "Emergency Broadcast System."

I pay the man close attention because he does not look happy. In fact he looks very upset, and in all my years of watching men with perfect suits and hair repeat news stories to me, I have never seen one look upset. Even his tie is crooked and looked upset.

"The National Guard, State, and Federal agencies have advised that everyone remain inside. The ash cloud is still growing, and there is no sure idea when it will pass."

I do not like the sounds of those words, but I keep listening and he keeps talking.

"Testing on the ash has been inconclusive as to its dangers. Medical agencies at this time do not know the extent of the content of the ash and warn that you do not breathe in any of the ash, or let it touch your skin."

I turn the sound down some as he starts into how far the road closures were extending, how far the ash cloud might drift, and so on. It seems clear to me that all my hoping and wishing and thoughts of doing a rain dance have done no good. The ash is continuing to fall, and no one really knows anything more.

The television goes back to the sign and then back to gray after a few minutes. I pull my maroon reading chair around so that it faces the window so I can watch the gray, lack of contrast show going on outside.

The falling flakes of ash seem hypnotic.

THREE

AT SOME POINT, those flakes must have put me to sleep, because when I wake up I have another surprise waiting for me. My window is completely covered in ash. And little bits of it are seeping in around the edges of the single pane window where normally only a draft and a few drops of water appear.

That surprises me.

That is the second time in two days I have woken up from a nap and been surprised.

Plus the fact that the power is still on surprises me.

Sort of a bonus surprise.

I have no upstairs in my small, one-bedroom house with a lean-to on the side for a garage. So I can not run up and see how deep the ash has gotten while I napped. But the clock on the wall says I have been asleep for two hours. Clearly ash falling is a very peaceful thing.

Around me the house creaks slightly, as if a wind is blowing outside. After two house creaks the alarm sounds softly on the television, startling me just like it had done before my nap when it was turned up loud.

After a few moments the man with the crooked tie comes back on. Only this time the tie is gone and his eyes look red. Clearly he needs a nap like I had just gotten.

He goes through the same speech he gave the last time I had listened. The ash continues, and is spreading. And from all aerial shots that they could get, which look very beautiful on television, the volcano continues to spew out ash at an ever increasing rate.

I stare at the beautiful blue sky around the volcano above the ash. It is a very sharp contrast to the gray outside my window.

I pay even more attention as the tie-less man gets to reports of the depth of the ash in certain places around the metropolitan area. With some of these numbers he cannot look at the camera, but instead just reads calmly.

He is like a doctor telling a patient he is about to die. When he gets to my area of town, and says that the depth of the ash

has reached forty feet and is continuing to build up, I know I am the patient.

I have been buried alive while I napped.

And my little house is my coffin.

Now that is a surprise I had never dreamed I would wake up to find.

Again the house creaks and adds in a groan. The man without a tie on the television says he will return in fifteen minutes. Before the alarm signaling the end of his little talk can end, the power goes off.

It seems that for the near future I will not be able to check on the progress of the man and his tie.

I sit in the dark for a moment, letting my eyes adjust to the lack of light, then move slowly to find the candles on my small kitchen table. The first match seems extra bright, and after a moment and three matches I have five candles burning, giving the house a warm feel, and a sulfur smell.

I look around deciding that I have to think about my house differently than a coffin. I have to think of it as a safe, warm cave.

Only my cave has a limited supply of oxygen and might collapse under the weight of the ash.

I stop the thought and make myself think of the house, lit by the orange glow of the flickering candles, as my cave.

I get settled on one of my two kitchen chairs, repeating the word "cave" over and over. I am in the fifth or sixth repetition when there is a huge crash and the area around me fills with swirling ash.

Thinking quickly, I lean forward over the table and shelter one candle and a box of matches as best I can.

Somehow I manage to keep the candle burning as the ash swirls like a gray river filling up a space.

The heat from the candle burns my neck a little, but I ignore that. And I try to ignore the bone-dry feel of the ash and the smell of rotting eggs that fills every sense I have.

I take slow, shallow breaths through my nose, trying not to let too much of the stuff into my lungs.

Slowly, so slowly, the stuff settles and I grow used to the smell.

I look up, using the one candle to see how the ash now coats everything I own with a layer of gray that makes all my things look faded.

The other candles have gone out, but moving slowly, so as to not swirl up too much more ash, I get two of them lit, giving me enough light to see the living room.

My big front window is smashed inward from the pressure of all that ash against it. My living room is full of ash, and the televisions are buried.

Around me the house creaks again, but nothing else happens. Maybe the window breaking open has relieved some pressure, but I didn't know how that might work. It is just the best positive thought I can come up with at the moment.

FOUR

I LOOK AROUND, staring at all the odd differences a thin layer of ash can make with things. My mirror still reflects, but it also scatters the light. The table is covered, but not much of the area under the table, leaving the faded green tile as a contrast.

Every corner in the place seems rounded by the ash, every edge dulled.

I slowly open my fridge, get out a red apple and a bottle of water, then take my three candles and crawl under my kitchen table. Now the next time something breaks and lets in more ash, I will be protected. The table is like a second home, giving me another roof over my head.

Suddenly, as if someone had stuck a feather down my throat, I cough. I manage to cough into the kitchen and away from the candles.

They stay lit.

Dust swirls with the cough.

The house creaks.

I lay down on the floor, on my back, trying not to cough again while staring at the underside of the kitchen table. It is a sight I had never expected to see. I would think that no one would ever expect to see the unfinished underside of a table by candle light. But still it has a beauty all its own as the flames give the surface odd shadows.

I focus on the shadows for a moment trying not to cough.

Then, while staring at the underside of the kitchen table, I think about washing my Rambler.

I can remember the feel of how much I had wanted rain today, how much I was angry at the rain the day before.

Now I have changed again. I don't want it to rain. Rain now will make the ash even heavier, and more than likely crush my poor little house.

For the third time in just two days, my feelings about rain have changed. Part of me is glad that I had never tripped on religion and prayed for rain, because I might have been successful.

And it was lucky I can't dance.

I laugh at the idea that my not being able to dance might save my life.

I yawn, while at the same time trying to not breathe in any of the dry ash still floating in the air.

I have no idea why I am so sleepy. Maybe there is a sleep drug in the ash. Maybe, after all this was over, they would shovel up the ash and put it in bottles and sell it to the rest of the world for a sleep-aid.

It would work well. I am getting very tired.

I yawn again, and then close my eyes.

Maybe, just maybe, a little nap might help.

Maybe the ash is doing me a favor, allowing me to sleep so that when I wake up there will be yet another surprise.

Maybe by then the power will be back on, and a wind will have come up and blown all the ash away, and then I can again hope for rain to help clean up the yard.

Surprises after naps are always interesting. I just have to think they are going to be good.

As I drift off into my nap, I yawn again and think about how much fun it will be to again wash my Rambler.

DEAN WESLEY
SMITH

USA Today BESTSELLING AUTHOR

*WARM
SPRINGS*

A THUNDER MOUNTAIN NOVEL

Belle returns to her old home town, looking for clues as to what happened to her great great grandmother a hundred years in the past.

Zane, on a secret mission into the past, never expects to meet the woman of his dreams.

A complex time travel novel that explores alternate realities, a future no one wants to face, and sets the Thunder Mountain universe going into the future.

WARM SPRINGS
A Thunder Mountain Novel

For Kris

PART ONE
The Institute

CHAPTER ONE

June 9th, 2020
Boise, Idaho

ISABELLE "BELLE" RUSSELL felt stunned by the sheer beauty of Warm Springs Avenue in Boise, Idaho. The massive old oak and cottonwood trees formed a dark green ceiling over the wide boulevard, letting the sun through in only streaks of brilliance.

On the right side of the road when leaving the downtown area, majestic stone and white-painted Victorian mansions sat back away from the road behind high hedges and wrought-iron gates. The rows of mansions with their high peaks overlooked the Boise River below and the Boise Valley and desert to the east.

The morning air was crisp, but held a promise of getting much warmer as the day went on. Boise was built on the edge of the high desert, sprawled along a river between the desert and towering mountains. Modern homes had crawled up the ridgelines of the foothills above the city like strings of lights draped over dark brown shapes.

Last night, all those lights had been something to see as she drove in her rented car from the airport into downtown Boise. But during the day, the brown of the foothills leading to pine trees much higher up the slopes was the dominant feature over the town.

From where she stood on the wide concrete sidewalk on Warm Springs Avenue, she could see neither the mountains behind her or much beyond glimpses of the huge mansions in front of her through the walls and hedges.

Down the avenue a half-mile closer to town was her family's old home, also a large mansion on the river's side of the avenue. She had stopped and stared at it for a time from her car, trying to get a peek of anything through the high hedge and fence. Maybe later she would go back there and talk to the owners.

She had dressed in layers for the morning. She had on jeans, her running shoes, a light white blouse with a sports bra under it, and for the chill this morning, she had pulled on a green Stanford sweatshirt. She was glad she had.

She had been born and raised in Phoenix, so anything that seemed the slightest bit cold sent chills through her. At the age of thirty-one, she had never gotten over that, even after being away from Phoenix except for visits for over a decade.

She had flown in last night from San Francisco, rented a car, and found her wonderful upscale hotel in the center of the city, just blocks from the lit-up capitol building that looked like a smaller duplicate of the one in Washington, DC.

At night, the capitol building's polished stones shone under the lights and the small park in front of it where a statue of a man standing on a pedestal gave the entire area a feeling of importance.

She had fallen into bed thirty minutes after arriving, tired from the last days of teaching for the spring semester at Stanford, and then the flight to Boise. But now, this morning, she felt much more refreshed and ready to enjoy herself, and with luck do some special research in a brand new place.

But most of all, she wanted to find out just what the Historical Studies Institute wanted of her. They said they had an offer and were willing to pay all expenses for her to come and listen to the offer.

She had agreed, if she could stay for a month and do some research and the institute had agreed at once and was willing to pick up the tab for the entire time. Considering she lived mostly on her teacher's salary and what little money her books brought in, that was a welcome relief.

But she would wait and see. It sounded almost too good to be true, and that bothered her more than she wanted to admit.

The breakfast in The Grand hotel had been wonderful and filling, with a light fruit salad, some freshly scrambled eggs, and toast. She then got her rental car out of valet parking and headed east out of town, eventually finding the large, five-lane avenue called Warm Springs.

It seemed the Historical Studies Institute occupied one of the huge Victorian mansions on the river's side.

That had surprised her. Clearly the institute had great funding. She would need to find out from where before she ever agreed to work with them on anything.

She had found parking on a side street that looked like a residential area built in the 1930s, and walked back to the institute carrying only her small black leather tablet case that also functioned as a purse. With its leather strap, it hung off her shoulder and never got in her way. Most of the time she felt that just carrying a tablet was easier than carrying a heavier laptop case.

A ten-foot tall hedge covering a stone wall, well maintained and recently trimmed, blocked her view of the institute from Warm Springs Avenue. The hedge had clearly grown for decades over a tall, river-stone wall.

She glanced at her watch. It was just nine in the morning mountain time. Pretty early for her, but she had wanted to get an early start, and could never sleep late while traveling anyway.

She managed to get across the five lane busy avenue and on the sidewalk in front of the institute grounds.

What looked like an extremely old metal plaque that was set into the stone in the hedge had the name of the institute on it and nothing more. Very stark and official looking, enough to make her wonder if she had even found the right place.

Scaring away unwanted guests was more than likely what the sign was for.

A wide wrought iron gate blocked a wide driveway to her left and a smaller metal gate blocked the sidewalk in front of her leading to the mansion. The

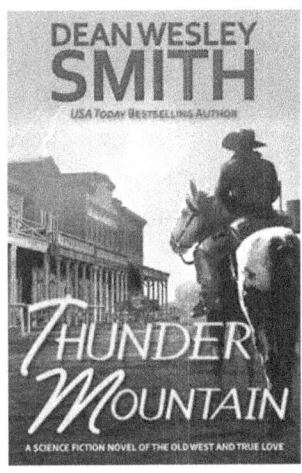

pedestrian gate had a more modern hours sign on it.

The hours were from 9 a.m. to 4 p.m. weekdays and Saturday. A buzzer and intercom stuck out of the thick green hedge beside the gate. She at least made it here during the open hours.

She rang the buzzer and waited, looking around the wonderful historic neighborhood. She would wager every building within her sight was on the historic register. What an amazing neighborhood. It must have really been something back at the turn of the 20th century.

It was still something now.

The intercom cracked and then a male voice said, "Good morning. Please state your name and your business with the institute."

"Isabelle Russell," she said leaning into the intercom. "I was invited to come talk to Director Parks about a position."

There was a long pause that made her wonder if she had been heard or if she had needed to push some unseen button somewhere. She was about to say something else when the male voice came back clearly.

"Welcome, Dr. Russell. It is an honor to have you visit our institute. Just follow the sidewalk up to the front door and come inside."

There was a buzz and the gate clicked open.

She felt slightly surprised at the suddenly warm welcome. Clearly they knew about her books and different degrees and areas of study since they had invited her here. But she wasn't often called Dr. Russell these days. Mostly, if anyone called her anything, it was professor.

She stepped through the gate and let it close and latch behind her.

As she did, it felt as if she had stepped into another world. The traffic noise on the busy street behind her dimmed to almost nothing.

Around her was one of the most beautiful and luscious green front lawns she had ever seen, accented in various flowerbeds. The lush green lawn flowed around the flowerbeds and the trunks of the massive old oak and cottonwood trees like a river around stones.

"Wow," she said out loud to herself as she studied the front area and then the large two-story Victorian mansion with a painted-white porch across the front. Two massive round towers reached for the blue sky up through the trees and large stone pillars held up the second floor above the porch.

"This place really, really has some funding," she said aloud.

And that sentence made her again wonder what they wanted from her.

The mansion had tall windows with drapes pulled open across the front to let in light. The driveway went past the mansion to the left and toward the back where she could see some other buildings all painted to match the white and stone of the main building.

A hedge over other walls ran along both sides of the massive estate, blocking anything but a view of the top floors and towers of the Victorian mansions on either side.

She went up the five stone steps and onto the wooden front porch, her tennis shoes making almost no sounds. Three different settings of furniture were grouped along the porch. The chairs were all period chairs and short couches that would be appropriate to when the mansion was built in the late 1980s. A wonderful touch of detail.

A couple of the settings had clearly been used recently. She stopped and looked back at the beautiful shaded yard. She would have no trouble at all sitting here sipping on an iced tea and just relaxing.

Not even the sounds of the traffic from the busy Warm Springs Avenue beyond got over that wall and into this sanctuary.

So what was this place?

And how in the world did they get so much funding? That question was going to drive her nuts until she got an answer.

She turned back to the big ornately carved front door with a bronze "Welcome" sign beside it.

Looked like she was about to find out.

CHAPTER TWO

June 9th, 2020
Boise, Idaho

LOGAN ZANE THOMAS had never expected to go to work today and meet the woman of his dreams. He had known that Dr. Russell was coming for the last few days, but he had not seen a picture of her, or even thought anything of meeting her except pure excitement.

One hundred years in the future, she was one of the most famous genetics experts there was, and today was her first visit to the institute. And he was here to meet her on her very first visit.

He couldn't believe his luck.

He did a quick real-time search on her just to make sure he wasn't mixing up details he knew about her from the future with where she was now at this moment in time. That would not be a good idea, especially since he was trying to stay undercover and not let anyone here know when he was from.

In his time, his name was Zane Logan, but in this time he went by Logan Zane Thomas.

He studied the computer screen in front of him quickly. Up until this point in time, Dr. Isabelle Russell taught at Stanford and had three well-respected books on the use of genetics and genealogy. Zane had read all three of them and enjoyed them.

He had also read numbers of her books that she hadn't written yet and enjoyed them as well.

In all his imagination, he would never have expected to be sitting here when she first came to the institute. She would become the founder of the genealogy section of this very institute, using genetics to track every human who had lived.

In his time, she was a legend. Considered a founder.

He was going to be honored beyond belief to meet her, and he sure hoped like hell he didn't screw this up. This was not at all what he expected to be doing here.

On the orders of the institute's director in 2120, he had come back secretly to this time and spent seven years establishing an identity here, including a number of degrees. His credentials and real specialty from his own time were in the research and exploration of various caves around the world.

In other words, he was a caver, maybe the best there was in 2120.

He had already written two books on the subject under this false name in this time, and he really wanted to go farther back in time at some point to find some of the lost caves that were only rumored to exist.

He had come from New York City to the institute here in Boise last fall to research a new book for a month, and they had offered to let him stay and he had taken them up on the offer.

Since he was spending so much time in the institute's massive library down near the Idaho Historical Center off Capitol Boulevard, he had asked Director Parks one day if he could help out in any other way.

Jesse Parks, the Institute Director, and the only one of the fourteen founding members of the institute that Zane had met so far, had hired him on the spot to work the front desk part time for far more money than the job was worth.

Zane didn't need the money. No one in the institute needed the money, but he most certainly wanted the job. It kept him on the front side of what was happening with the institute without actually being invited downstairs into the caverns yet.

He wasn't supposed to know about the huge caverns under this building.

Most days, he just sat in the big front room of the old mansion at a large desk and not a person came through the door. A big glass chandelier dominated the center of the room hanging from the high ceiling. The reception desk was an antique and sat in the archway leading into a formal dining room behind the desk.

Dark wood trim and light paint on the textured wall gave the room a feeling of seriousness, like a library. The wall of old leather books across from the massive stone fireplace didn't hurt the feeling at all.

This room looked almost exactly the same one hundred years in the future in his time.

As he sat at the desk facing the front door, to his left was a grand staircase made of polished dark mahogany that led to the offices upstairs. In front of him and to his right was a massive stone fireplace

with a large seating area in front of it on an area rug over the polished pine floors.

The furniture was period to the house's building and was actually very comfortable.

The reason Director Parks gave for hiring Zane was that Director Parks wanted someone with a historical background and some credentials to greet whoever came through the front door.

So Zane and a guy named Boone traded off the hours the institute allowed visitors. Boone was doing research on the old small-town newspapers of the Old West and seemed like a nice-enough guy. But Zane knew he would never actually be part of the institute, never invited below.

When no one came through the door, which was most of the time, they were both free to use a major research computer at the front desk to work.

Now Zane quickly put away his notes in a drawer and shut down the research computer as he heard Dr. Russell's footsteps on the porch. He quickly hit a hidden buzzer to let Director Parks in his office upstairs know Dr. Russell was about to come in.

Zane forced himself to take a deep breath and calm down. This wasn't the famous Dr. Russell who started an entire arm of the institute over the next ten years. This was a real human being from this time, and he needed to be careful, just as those traveling from this time back to 1900 needed to be careful.

Dr. Russell hesitated on the front porch as Zane remembered doing his first time through that door a hundred years in the future. He moved around from behind the desk to greet her as she pushed the big wooden front door open.

She didn't really see him at first, since she was glancing around at the wonderful mansion front room, the carved wood-work, and the big crystal chandelier that hung in the middle of the room.

Zane suddenly found that he couldn't breathe.

He had been nervous to start, but now that changed to something much stronger.

Dr. Russell had long beautiful brown hair that she had pulled back away from her face so that it cascaded down her back.

She had dark brown eyes and beautiful skin that seemed to almost glow. She was wearing a green Stanford sweatshirt and jeans and carrying a small tablet case over her shoulder on a long leather strap.

From the looks of her thin frame and the style of tennis shoes, she was clearly a runner.

Zane forced himself to take a deep breath and get hold of his mind again. He had been around his share of beautiful women in his life. His ex-wife had done modeling around the New York area in his time before he joined the institute.

But there was just something special about Dr. Russell that Zane was instantly attracted to.

Not like him at all. In fact, since coming to this time and then moving to Boise, he hadn't even had any dates. His research and building his cover and his regular trips to major cave formations had kept him busy. His only relaxation had been to learn to ski last winter at a nearby ski area.

He had been nervous to start, but now that changed to something much stronger.

"Welcome to the institute, Dr. Russell," he managed to say, stepping forward with his hand out.

He was damn glad his voice didn't squeak.

His words seemed to bring her back from staring around at the room and she smiled and looked into his eyes.

And then she seemed to freeze for a second as they held each other's gaze.

He was back having trouble breathing again.

Damn, what the hell was going on? She was going to be a founder of this institute. He couldn't be in lust with her. He just couldn't.

But he was.

She finally took his hand and it felt like a jolt of electricity had gone through him. He had never had this kind of attraction to a woman before in his memory.

She glanced down at their hands together and then back into his eyes.

Clearly she felt something as well.

Wow. He really needed to get hold of himself here before he screwed something up royally.

Finally, she shook his hand and let go, which disappointed him. Her wonderful skin felt fantastic against his.

"Thank you," she said, managing to nod.

Her face had flushed slightly and he had a hunch his face was flushed as well. It seemed they both clearly had a reaction to the other one.

Weird.

And nice.

Damn nice.

He pointed to a seating area in front of the big desk that had a large couch, three overstuffed period chairs that went with the age of the mansion, and a wooden polished coffee table. The seating area filled the area in front of the large stone fireplace.

"Director Parks will be down in a minute," Zane said. "In the meantime, can I get you something to drink? Water, tea, coffee are the options."

She shook her head without looking back at him, as if she was afraid to. "Thank you, but I think I'm okay at the moment."

As far as he was concerned, she was more than okay. She was flat stunning. Brilliant, a legend, and stunningly good-looking. How was that possible?

As she sat down in one of the big chairs, her tablet case tucked beside her, he said, "My name is Logan Zane Thomas, but everyone just calls me Zane."

Her head snapped up like he had shouted fire or something. Her eyes were actually seeing him it seemed for the first time as he dropped onto the couch.

"Dr. Logan Thomas?" she asked. "The caver?"

He nodded. "But I hate that Dr. stuff. Makes me sound like I should be doing prostate exams or something."

Thank God she laughed at his stupid joke, a wonderful laugh that seemed to just float in the room for a moment.

"I hate it as well," she said. "But not because I don't like prostate exams. Please just call me Belle."

Zane laughed and said. "I walked into that one. I sure enjoyed your books. You are doing some groundbreaking work in combining genetics with genealogy."

"And I enjoyed your books as well," she said, smiling. "Do you really also have advanced degrees in geology, historical library research, and physical training?"

Zane managed to at least nod. "Far too much time in school," he said. In his time he actually had two other degrees besides those areas, but those three were set for cover in this time. "Although I got through a few of them at the same time."

"Yeah, I did the same," she said, smiling.

The silence between them filled the big room for a moment before Zane finally got himself back on the institute script that he was supposed to attempt to follow with someone new coming in.

"I need to ask what you think the institute can do to help you?" Zane said.

She smiled. "Director Parks called me here to interview for something," she said. "Paid my way. So here I am."

She smiled at Zane, staring into his eyes. Damn, he could sit and stare into her eyes for a very long time if she would let him.

"But besides whatever the institute is offering, I have a twofold reason to come here," she said, finally seeming to get up enough nerve to tell him. "I have heard the institute has vast resources to help historical researchers with projects of various kinds."

"It does," Zane said, nodding. "I've been here since last fall doing research on historical lost caves for a new book and haven't begun to use all of what is available."

"I am not rich," Belle said. "So I would need to know how much spending time in various forms of research would cost."

Now Available
from all your favorite booksellers
in trade paper and electronic editions.

"Nothing," Zane said, "if you are approved, and considering they asked you to come, that seems very likely. And the institute wants no credit or anything else from your work. The institute exists to help historians such as ourselves to get our facts right."

He was very proud of himself for not slipping there, since he knew for a fact that if he didn't blow this, she would be here at the institute for a very long time to come.

She seemed to be taken back by that. "This place must have some serious funding."

He laughed. "It must, but I have no idea what it might be."

There were some things he flat had to lie about instead of just twist the truth, and the funding was one area. The institute had vast resources. Money was easy when you traveled in time and knew what was going to happen.

"So what is your second reason for coming here?" he asked, trying to stay focused on what she said and not her fantastic eyes and beautiful smile.

She again looked uncomfortable. "It is a personal research reason."

He nodded, indicating she should give more details if she wanted.

"My great, great, grandfather died here in Boise in 1930," Belle said, "right after the birth of his first grandchild. He is buried in an old cemetery here, from what I have discovered."

Zane watched her. Clearly as an historian, this personal quest bothered her and he wasn't sure why.

"A week after my great, great, grandfather died, my grandmother told her son that she was going up to a place called Monumental Summit Lodge to get away. It seems she and her husband had run it

for years. She got on a horse and vanished into history."

Zane nodded. "And you would like to try to discover what happened to her?"

"It is a great family mystery that has been handed down over time," she said. "That family secret drove me to get degrees in genealogy and another in genetics to try to track her. It is the reason I do what I do, actually."

"Wow," Zane said. He hadn't known that about her.

"But my great, great grandparents seemed to have no parents that I can find ahead of arriving at the lodge," Belle said, "and my great, great grandmother vanished into the same thin air after her husband died. What happened to her and where they both came from before the lodge has driven my family crazy for a very long time."

"And clearly driven you to entire areas of study that are now life passions," Zane said. He could understand her desire to solve that mystery. It actually sounded fascinating in many ways.

"It sure has," she said. "I'm now slowly becoming a leading expert in the new field of genealogy and the application of genetics in historical searches."

Zane nodded. He didn't want to tell her that in his time she was the founder of that entire branch of science.

"The records of the institute are amazingly complete," Zane said, "especially concerning the area around Boise and the Pacific Northwest. I am sure you will find some help in them. What was the name of your great, great, grandmother?"

"Dawn Edwards Rogers," Belle said. "Her husband's name was Madison Rogers."

Zane somehow managed to not jerk or fall over backwards or even make a motion. Her grandparents were two of the founders of the institute. They were legends as well.

Thank heavens Belle was looking at the fireplace when she told him their names.

He took a deep breath and nodded.

Upstairs, he heard a slight thump from Director Parks' office. He sure hoped the director would continue to take his time coming down. Zane was enjoying talking with Belle.

Even though her very presence scared him to death.

CHAPTER THREE

June 9th, 2020
Boise, Idaho

BELLE WAS STUNNED at her reaction to Zane Thomas. She had spent five years with the same man, another professor at Stanford named Ben, but that had ended a few years back. She had had her share of dates before and after leaving Ben, and otherwise she had no real interest in much else on a relationship front. Her research and books were her passion.

So a reaction of almost lust levels toward a colleague was unusual for her to say the least. But damn, Zane was handsome.

He looked to be about her age and had black hair cut short and dark eyes that seemed intense and full of fun at the same time. He laughed easily, which made his square face come alive.

He had wide shoulders and considering he spent time climbing in caves, he had to be very strong and amazingly brave. He wore a blue dress shirt with the sleeves rolled up, regular jeans, and running shoes.

And that handshake had actually taken her breath away. How the hell was that possible?

It was everything she could do to not stare at him like a lovesick high school girl.

What the hell was a man like him, with as many degrees as he had and two well-received books out, working at a front desk of a research institute? This place was getting more and more intriguing by the moment.

She had done her share of amateur cave exploring over the years, and no car she was in could pass a tourist cave without stopping and spending a few hours underground on a tour.

So she had been a fan of Zane and his books for the last few years. And now just felt stunned to meet him.

"I'm fairly certain that in the institute records are details about your distant grandmother." Zane smiled. "Forgot how many greats in front of grandmother there were."

"Two," she said.

At that moment, she heard footsteps on the wood of the grand staircase behind Zane, and he turned around and stood.

She stood as well as a man with short brown hair came down the stairs. He was also about their age and was also in great shape. But she had no real attraction to him, even though he was great looking as well.

He reached the bottom of the stairs and smiled. "Wonderful having you here, Dr. Russell," the man said, coming around the couch with his hand extended. "Thanks for coming. My name is Jesse Parks. I am the institute's director."

"Wonderful meeting you, Director," Belle said. "Please just call me Belle."

"Be glad to," Parks said. "I hope your trip was uneventful."

"Very nice, and thank you for the nice hotel as well," she said.

He nodded. "I understand from what you told Zane that you have a twofold reason to ask to use our research facilities beside our offer for a position. Your own research and your family research. Is that correct?"

Zane looked slightly startled. Clearly he had not known the director was going to blurt out that the room was monitored. Belle found that charming and relaxing, actually. And revealing it to a perspective employee was a logical business practice.

"I am," she said. "I have heard that this institute can really help me with my main field of research in historical genetics. The family research is just a side puzzle for me. But a very important one."

"And I hope your research will continue on in the same area as your first three books," Parks said.

"I hope to do that for some time as well," she said. "But finding the time around my teaching schedule is always an issue."

Parks nodded. "Time we might be able to help with."

Zane nodded to that as well.

Belle had no idea what he meant, but decided to wait and ask later on that, after she found out why they had asked her to come here. And how this place was funded.

"We would very much like you to join the researchers here at the institute on your private projects," Parks said. "The kind of work and research you have been doing is exactly what we are the most interested in helping. Then later this afternoon or tomorrow, after you get

settled, we can talk about the reason we asked you to come here. And be assured that even if you decline our offer, you will still be free to research as freely as you would like for as long as you would like."

Belle felt stunned. "Thank you. I am honored."

"We only have a simple, but binding, nondisclosure agreement for you to sign about what you see here. But past that, any research or work you do here is completely yours. And we would prefer that you not thank us or even give us credit in any fashion."

She nodded again, even more stunned. "I will comply without an issue to those terms."

Parks smiled and stood, again extending his hand.

Belle and Zane both stood and Belle shook the director's hand again.

"Welcome aboard the research side of things, Dr. Russell. I mean, Belle. We will talk later this afternoon or tomorrow after you are settled about the main reason for your visit."

"That sounds fine," she said, smiling. And it did. Nice to actually have people not in a hurry all the time. "It is an honor to be on board."

"I'm going to assign Zane here to show you all the ropes and where things are located," Parks said.

He then turned to Zane. "I'll cover the front here while you help Belle find her way around. She needs to get a place to live I assume, get her passwords and such, if you don't mind."

"Be glad to help," Zane said, nodding and then smiling at Belle.

Belle just hoped her face wasn't red, because she liked the idea of Zane helping her more than she wanted to admit.

"I have an odd request," Parks said, turning to Belle one more time.

She nodded. "I'll do what I can."

"I would prefer if you started your first research here with your great, great, grandmother's disappearance. It would help in a way you will understand later."

Of all the things that Parks could have asked, that surprised her more than she wanted to admit.

"I would be glad to do that," she said, nodding.

"And please, include Zane in your research on that topic if you don't mind. Again the reason will become clear later."

"I wouldn't mind in the slightest," she said. "Having another researcher help me with that mystery would be wonderful."

"And it sounds damn interesting to me," Zane said. "Glad to help."

Parks nodded and smiled. "Zane, help her get settled here in Boise. Institute apartments are very nice and there are four still open. And give her the tour of this place and the main library as you get started with the research. I'll check in with you both later to see how it's going and see if it's time to talk."

With that, he turned and headed for the staircase.

All Belle could do was stand there beside Zane as they both stared at the director's back.

She had been through her share of job interviews, but never one that started like that.

CHAPTER FOUR

June 9th, 2020
Boise, Idaho

ZANE JUST SMILED to himself at what had just happened. He wondered if someone from his time had come back and given hints to Director Parks about the importance of getting Belle into the institute. That sort of thing was against all rules, but it sure seemed likely in this case.

Zane still felt stunned that he was here when Belle walked through the door for the first time.

And there was no way in the world that he was complaining in any fashion that he got to spend time with her. The chance to get to know Belle personally was a dream as far as he was concerned.

She just took his breath away every time he looked at her.

Plus, she was one of the very few people that had read his books and seemed to know who he was. Only cavers knew him at all, so clearly she must have an interest in caving which he would have to find out about at some point.

"Well, looks like Boise is going to be home for a time," Zane said turning to Belle after Parks vanished up the stairs. "You'll like it I'm sure. Not as urban as the area around Stanford, but it has its charms."

"Looking forward to it," Belle said. "Since many of my historical family lived here. But I don't have that much of a budget to stay too long. Professor's salaries are just not that high and my books do all right, but nothing to shout home about. And I have no idea what the institute is offering yet."

Zane laughed. "Here comes the first in a long line of surprises about this place. The apartments Parks mentioned are free to anyone accepted to use the institute for research, as you were just accepted."

He loved the look on her beautiful face. Stunned and puzzled.

"You are kidding?"

"I have more than enough money from a family trust, but they won't let me pay for them either," Zane said. "Three bedrooms, furnished, all utilities paid, and they look more like condominiums than apartments by a long ways. Plus they are within walking distance of here down along the river path."

"Wow," was all she could say.

"Do you have a rental car?" he asked.

She nodded and again he smiled at her.

"Second surprise. One of the buildings around back of this mansion has institute cars free for all researchers to use. So we're going to need to get your rental car turned back in today."

She again shook her head. "And I suppose you are going to say that food is free as well."

"Third surprise."

"You have got to be kidding," she said, laughing. "I am dreaming still, right?"

"Nope," Zane said. "I felt the same way. I came here to research historical caves in the west and they invited me to stay and work on my research for as long as I wanted. Wait until you see the library and research facilities. They will knock your socks off."

He smiled at the shocked look on her beautiful face, then turned and headed back over to his desk to start up the paperwork. He had only done this for two others before, so he hoped he would get it right.

"And the institute is just giving me all this and expecting nothing in return?" Belle asked sort of stumbling over and taking a seat in a chair in front of Zane's desk.

"This place honestly just wants to help you do your research and write your books," Zane said as he fired up his administrative computer. "Nothing more. Now that's a dream I haven't woken up from yet either."

"But why?" Belle said.

"When you find out the answer to that question, please tell me," Zane said, bringing up the nondisclosure agreement.

He needed to make sure he remained in character. And his character was a worker here who knew nothing of the real affairs of this place.

He hit print and then faced her. "See why they don't want you telling anyone about this place except in general terms?"

"I'm starting to understand," Belle said, nodding.

He slipped her the one sheet agreement and watched as she read it.

Damn she was stunning and smart and clearly in shape. She carefully read the short document twice, then shrugged and looked up at him. "Nothing I can see wrong at all."

"I could find nothing wrong with it either," Zane said. "And that's the only document. No other agreements at all. You just can't tell anyone at all what you see and experience here."

A hundred years in the future, the agreement was still almost identical. It seemed the institute never had needed more.

She took a pen that was lying on the desk near her and signed the nondisclosure and dated it.

Zane quickly made a copy of it and put the copy in an envelope and handed it back to her. He put the original in a tray labeled with Director Parks' name.

"It will take me just a minute to get you into the system and print out your card," Zane said.

He turned to the computer so that she was to his right, and then as he went, he asked her a number of questions, including the exact spelling of her name, emergency contact numbers, her cell phone number, and so on. He could feel her sitting there watching him and he honestly liked that.

After about two minutes, he went back over the simple form to make sure he hadn't missed anything, then hit print.

To one side of the dining room behind his desk, a hidden printer started up. He stood and went to it and got her an institute ID card. It was the size of a credit card and had nothing but the letters HRI in gold script on one side and her name printed under the large initials. The backside of the card was blank, not even a bar code or scanning code.

He went back to his desk and handed it to her. "That's the golden key to everything. I'll show you how it works as we go. If it wears out or you lose it, we can easily get you a new one right here."

She looked at it for a moment. "I think I have said before that I am beyond stunned."

"I know the feeling exactly," Zane said. And he did. He remembered sitting there looking at his institute card in the same way. "So let me direct until you get your feet back under you."

"Direct away," she said, smiling.

"First, we take your rental car back to the airport," he said. "Then we show you an apartment I am sure you are going to love and get you moved out of the hotel."

"I love the sounds of that," she said.

"And at some point we'll come back here and give you a tour of this place," Zane said, deciding to leave that until she was far more settled.

She glanced around at the big front room of the mansion. "I would like that very much."

If she was stunned at getting free room and food and transportation, she was really going to be shocked to learn about the three massive floors under this building that were the real heart of the institute.

Zane stood and indicated Belle should come with him to the front door. "We're headed out, Director," Zane called up the stairs.

But Director Parks didn't answer. More than likely he was on the phone or had gone out the back or down under the building.

You just never knew around here, the way people were coming and going all the time. It was an amazing place.

And now, with Belle here as well, it had just gotten even better.

CHAPTER FIVE

June 9th, 2020
Boise, Idaho

BELLE HAD ZANE drive her rental car through the morning traffic back out to the airport. She had only been inside the institute for an hour and she had a hunch that hour was going to change her life. And that had her somewhat rattled.

As they got going, it was clear Zane was a great driver, and not in any hurry at all. He gave her a running tour of Boise on the way out Capitol Boulevard, past the old Union Pacific Train station that sat on a hill facing the Capitol building. He clearly had grown to love the town after coming here from New York for the institute.

He said he missed New York more than he wanted to admit at times, but the lifestyle of Boise was growing on him.

She had no doubt she was going to miss the San Francisco area this summer as well. But unlike Zane, she planned to go back in the fall. Zane said he planned on staying right here for as long as he could imagine doing research.

When she looked at him funny, he laughed and said, "You'll understand why shortly. As I said, the library and facilities are beyond belief. And the living is mostly free."

"I'm still having a hard time grasping that," she said.

"Still knocks me down at times as well," he said, laughing.

They dropped off her rental car and caught a cab back to an apartment complex near the river.

Actually, from what little she could see of it, the complex looked far, far more upscale than any apartment complex she had ever seen. In fact, she had no doubt this was a high-level condominium complex built next to the river.

He paid for the cab as they climbed out in the shaded parking lot of the complex. She thanked him and he just said it was no big deal.

"But wait until you see this place," he said, indicating she should follow him toward buildings hidden among pine and oak and willow trees and among flower beds filled with various flowers of different colors.

It was now almost eleven and the sun was warming up the air and making the sweatshirt just too much.

She pulled it off and tucked it under her arm as they walked along a winding sidewalk. From what she could tell, each building was made of dark-painted wood and were two stories like a suburban home, only with fences and trees between each building. It quickly became clear that each building was only one unit.

The parking lot for the building had very few cars in it and spread for a long distance along the buildings. And the buildings seemed to be scattered and staggered along a hillside over the river so that each one would have a private deck to sit and look out over the river.

"My place is building #8," Zane said, pointing to the right as they reached a junction in the wide sidewalk and turned away from where he had pointed. "I booked you into building #14 if you want to take it."

"I thought you said these were apartments," she said, shaking her head at the beauty and tranquility of walking under the trees past the well-maintained lawns and shrubs and private two-story homes.

"Surprise number four," he said, laughing. "But that's what everyone at the institute calls these places. I kid you not."

"Places like this would rent in my area for far more than my annual salary," she said as they turned on a private sidewalk leading under more trees and to a building.

"They wouldn't be cheap in this city either," Zane said. "But the institute wants us researchers to be comfortable in all ways while we work."

"I'm still dreaming," she said. "But promise me you won't pinch me and wake me up."

"I'd be afraid I would wake myself up," Zane said, reaching the large carved wood front door and stepping aside.

She looked at him, puzzled.

"Your card opens your door," he said. "Mine wouldn't work here."

She fumbled at her small tablet carrier and pulled out the institute card, its gold letters over her name seeming to glow.

"Face up," Zane said and pointed to an almost unseen slot beside the door. "Slide it in and take it out."

She did as Zane said and heard a click.

Zane indicated she should go in.

She tucked her key back in her bag and pushed the large carved wood door open and stepped inside.

The entryway was about the size of a small bedroom and had brown stone floors, tall ceilings, and a large mirror on one wall across from a closet clearly used for coats and boots.

There was also a bench and a stand to put keys and such with fresh flowers on the stand.

An archway from the entry area showed a sunken furnished living room, a massive stone fireplace to one side, and a view out over the river that was worth more than Belle wanted to think about.

"Welcome home, Dr. Russell," a soft female voice said. "Welcome Dr. Thomas. If there is anything I can get for either of you, please just ask."

"Thank you, Goldie," Zane said.

She looked at Zane as the door behind them closed automatically with a click.

"The complex is called The Gold Rush Village," Zane said, smiling. "So the computer that looks out for all of our places we all call Goldie."

"Not monitored or recorded in here?" Belle asked, suddenly worried.

"I was worried about the same thing at first," Zane said. "So I had a tech guy at the institute who was here before me and also lives here, run me through the system. If you ask for something to be done or shout for help, you will get a response. Otherwise there are no cameras, no re-cording devices, nothing. Just a computer system guarding us all and taking care of the houses."

"Wow," she said. "Yet another surprise."

"We're just getting started," Zane said, laughing.

And for some reason, that was starting to worry her.

CHAPTER SIX

June 9th, 2020
Boise, Idaho

ZANE LET BELLE explore her new home while he sat in one of the big cloth chairs in the living room. The ceiling in here was high, with wide windows looking out over the river beyond.

There were three large overstuffed chairs, a love seat, and a couch in the living room, with a stone fireplace dominating one side of the room. Everything, including the soft carpet and drapes, was done in various brown tones that seemed to complement the wood trim and the dark wood deck beyond the window.

After a few minutes, Belle joined him, coming back down the open wood staircase and going through the living room and to the state-of-the-art kitchen on the other side of the living room.

She didn't say a word.

Zane doubted there was much she could say.

The kitchen had a counter with bar stools. The counter was open and looked out over the living room. A polished wood dining table with four chairs was tucked to one side of the kitchen in an alcove with windows that also looked out at the river.

The granite counters seemed to match the stone of the fireplace and the cabinets were also a light brown.

This place was almost identical to his place, just flipped so that his kitchen was on the other side.

Finally Belle came down the two steps into the sunken living room and dropped into a chair beside him facing the river. He just stared at her beautiful face and long brown hair and trim body as she looked out over the river.

He let the silence just last, since more than likely she needed time to gather her thoughts.

Finally, she looked away from the view and turned in her chair to face him. "You are saying this place is mine to use while I am doing my research?"

"It is," he said, doing his best to not get lost in her wonderful gaze. "I've added some personal details to my place and some pictures of caves I have explored and such on the walls, but past that my place looks almost the same as here."

"Why three bedrooms?" she asked.

Zane shrugged. "Guess if you have guests or something. Each bedroom in mine has its own bathroom."

"Yeah, up there as well," she said, pointing up to where the three bedrooms were. "So what's the limits on staying here?"

He shrugged. "Honestly, I don't think there are any, but you could ask Director Parks. I'll be going on a year this fall and never thought to ask him, to be honest."

She nodded and looked back at the river.

"So you like it?" he asked. "Would you want to live here while doing your research? The main library is about a half mile along the path, up river to the right."

"I like it more than I want to think about liking it," she said. "I've been trained to think that something too good to be real usually is too good to be real."

Zane nodded. He understood that completely. There was no doubt she was concerned about the funding of all this and sooner, rather than later, she was going to need a real explanation of the money behind the institute.

"I decided that until they dropped the other shoe," Zane said, "I was going to take advantage of the opportunity to work on my next book."

"So why were you working the front desk?" she asked, turning again to face him.

"Honestly," he said, "Director Parks said he needed people with credentials to greet new arriving guests. I am free to research from a computer there, and since only about three people a week come through the door, it didn't get in the way at all. And he pays me more than I would make teaching for sitting there for fifteen or so hours per week."

"Wow," she said, laughing. "And it makes sense, actually. It sure impressed me when someone of your credentials greeted me."

"Now you're just blowing smoke," he said laughing and trying not to show how happy he was that she thought he was impressive. "No one usually knows anything about me or my work. So you must be a fan of caving."

She looked into his eyes and nodded. "Very much, but haven't had the time or the money to do much besides a few tourist caves."

"Maybe that can change," he said.

Now Available
from all your favorite booksellers
in trade paper and electronic editions.

He then stood. "Let's go get you checked out of that hotel and your stuff back here and then get some lunch."

"Going to need to buy food and things like that later on," she said, as she stood as well.

"Grocery store about a block down the river. Your institute card gets you anything you want there for free."

"You have got to be kidding me?" she asked. Then she laughed. "I am saying that a lot, aren't I?"

"I am not kidding," he said. "I agree that this all seems to be too good to be true. But so far, it is true."

"Wow, does this place have some serious funding or what," she said, following Zane toward the door.

That he could not disagree with.

And when she discovered why, it would make sense.

If she accepted that time travel existed.

CHAPTER SEVEN

June 9th, 2020
Boise, Idaho

BELLE SAT ACROSS a wooden table from Zane in the moderately crowded Brooks Garden Restaurant just after noon. Around them plants and wooden barriers gave each table a sense of privacy even though the place was full of people taking lunch breaks from their offices. The high ceilings and the barriers and enough plants and small trees to start a greenhouse kept the noise down.

She instantly loved the place more than she wanted to admit. The smell of garlic and fresh baking bread seemed to just drift between the trees and plants and made her mouth water. She was hungry, more than she had thought.

"This place seems great," Belle said as they got seated. "And it smells wonderful."

"One of my favorite places," Zane said. "It takes the institute card as well without so much as a blink of the eye. But it's the longest walk from the institute of any of the restaurants that take the card, but that I don't mind."

"So how do you keep in shape here for the caving while you are doing the research?" she asked, staring into his dark eyes.

He shrugged. "That path along the river is wide and a fantastic running path, so I try to get out running most days for a few miles. Clears out the cobwebs on the research problems. And I do a lot of walking. And the apartment complex has a weight room I use a few times a week. How about you?"

"I try to run every day," she said. "And I think I'm going to enjoy the fewer hills here."

A waiter came and took their order, then she and Zane chatted about their research and the books they were working on until lunch was served. Belle had ordered a Cobb salad and fresh, soft breadsticks came with that smothered in butter. The salad was larger than anyone could ever eat alone, but she was so hungry, she planned on making a decent dent in it.

Zane ordered a chef's salad and it was just as big, if not bigger.

"So do you enjoy teaching?" Zane asked.

She shrugged. "It's a job and they let me alone to do research on my off time.

But it swallows a lot of time and energy. I wish my books would just pay my way at some point."

Zane looked up from his salad at that, slightly surprised. "I would have guessed you enjoyed it."

"Oh, I did for the first few years," she said. "But all my attention is on the books now. And working on the genetics and genealogy side of things. That's really starting to become important to me, so I get distracted."

"Know that feeling," Zane said, nodding.

After a moment of silence as they ate, Zane glanced up at her again. "Mind if I ask a personal question?"

"Since we're going to be researching my family together," she said, laughing, "I don't think any question is off limits."

Besides, she really wanted to get to know Zane and she wanted him to get to know her as well. She had only met him this morning, but she could tell already the attraction was very real.

"You married or have a boyfriend?" Zane asked, then quickly went back to eating.

"Nope," she said, laughing and happy that he had asked that question bluntly. "I was serious for a few years with a guy after I started teaching, but that's been over for a few years now. Never married. How about you?"

"Married once," he said. "Way back in undergrad. No kids. The marriage lasted a couple of bumpy years before we decided to go back to being friends. Now I'm an eccentric uncle to her two kids with her second husband."

Belle was thrilled that he was single. And he seemed to be pretty happy that she was as well. She decided to just take a more direct approach.

"So when your babysitting duties with me are finished, are there rules at the institute about researchers fraternizing?"

He looked up and smiled at her and her heart damn near joined her salad in her stomach.

"No rules that I know of," he said, smiling that smile she could really, really come to enjoy.

"In fact, the institute has very few rules except that we don't tell anyone about the place. And I don't feel like a babysitter in the slightest. Just a colleague who hopes to get to know you better."

She loved the sound of that answer more than she wanted to admit.

"So, colleague," she said, smiling at him. "Where would you suggest we go from here after lunch?"

"I was thinking that if you have records of where your great, great grandfather was buried, we go visit a grave and get started that way," he said. "You can often get all kinds of information from the other graves around an historical grave. Then we go back to the institute and look around there and talk more with Director Parks."

"Sounds perfect," she said. "I have the name of the cemetery. So do you want to tell the director our plans?"

Zane shrugged and said, "Might as well." He pulled out a cell phone. A moment later he was talking with Parks, giving him an update of the morning and their plans.

She watched him talk, not really listening, but instead just studying his handsome features, the slight shadow of beard growth, the shape of his ears, everything.

She had no idea why she was so attracted to Zane, but she sure was.

After a moment, Zane hung up and put his phone away.

"One of the founding members of the institute is going to pick us up out front in fifteen minutes," Zane said, sounding sort of shocked, "since we don't have a car. And take us to the cemetery, then back to the institute."

"Wow," Belle said. "Who is it?"

"Honestly," Zane said, "Parks didn't give me her name and I have never met any of the founding members of the institute. Until that conversation, I didn't even know there were any, since from what I thought, the institute was founded way back around 1880 or something."

"Hard to be a founding member wouldn't it?" Belle asked, looking at the puzzled look on Zane's face.

"More than likely I heard him wrong, but your arrival here has certainly triggered a bunch of stuff," he said. "I have never heard of anyone, myself included, that didn't take days to be accepted into the institute."

"I thought that was fast," she said. "So Director Parks did not make it a habit to come talk to interested researchers the first time?"

"You are the first," Zane said, shaking his head and taking a final bite of his salad before pushing it away.

"I wonder why I caused such a stir," Belle said. She really was worried about that. She had been invited, she knew that, for some job offer. But still, this seemed fast and sort of puzzling.

And she was still very worried that all this seemed just far too good to be true. What had she accidently tripped into?

"I say we take the direct approach and just ask the director when we get back what is bothering you," Zane said.

"I love that direct approach idea," Belle said. "In more things than just the institute."

He laughed and clearly agreed.

She took one last bite of the wonderful buttered breadstick and then pushed her salad and the breadsticks away. "I think we better get a bill and head out front. We don't want to make this mystery woman wait."

"A founding member," Zane said, smiling at her and laughing. "She's got to be almost too old to drive at this point."

"You would think," Belle said, laughing.

He laughed as well, smiling at her.

Damn she loved that smile of his.

CHAPTER EIGHT

June 9th, 2020
Boise, Idaho

ZANE AND BELLE were standing near the front door of the restaurant near the valet parking. The road in front of the restaurant was four lanes and one way and busy now during the lunch hour.

Zane had used his institute card to pay for the lunch and add a tip to show Belle what her card could do as well. The cashier hadn't even blinked an eye. It was as if he was taking a regular credit card.

Director Parks saying that a founding member of the institute was going to pick them up had him very worried. He knew, from his history and research coming back here from the future, that there were fourteen founding members, one of whom was Parks.

But in nine months on the surface of the institute in this time, he had not met or seen any of the others. So this was going to get interesting very quickly.

And he was going to have to be very careful.

After just a minute of standing near the front door, a white Cadillac SUV pulled up and a passenger side window rolled down and the woman behind the wheel motioned for them to jump in.

Zane was fairly convinced this was not an institute car, since in the large parking garage behind the institute building, he had never seen a Cadillac.

"Shotgun," Belle said as they headed across the sidewalk toward the car.

"Damn, you're fast," he said, laughing, and she climbed into the front seat and he climbed into the back, searching for the seat belt.

Belle extended her hand to the driver. "I'm Belle Russell."

"Just call me Dawn for now," the driver said, shaking Belle's hand and staring into Belle's eyes. "You would not believe how happy I am to meet you, Belle."

Belle said nothing, but Zane could tell she was rattled a little.

"I'm Zane," Zane said as he clicked in his seatbelt, managing to control his excitement and keep it out of his voice. "But I suppose you know that from what Director Parks told me."

The driver was a woman about his and Belle's age and had long brown hair pulled back and tied. She seemed trim and was wearing tennis shoes, jeans, and a t-shirt with some writing on the front that Zane couldn't read.

If this really was a founding member as the director had said, then their driver was Dawn Rogers Madison.

She was Belle's lost great, great grandmother, the very person Belle had come to research.

Zane was almost shaking from excitement.

Dawn Roger's first trip back in time was legendary in the institute and used as a story to illustrate how dying in a past timeline did not actually kill you.

Dawn got the big SUV back out into traffic and headed through town, turning west at one point.

"Nice meeting you finally, Zane," Dawn said. "So what did Jesse say about me, anyway," the woman asked, smiling over her shoulder at Zane.

"Just that you were one of the founding members of the institute," Zane said. "Nothing more."

Zane didn't dare say anything more or show any reaction if this really was Dawn Rogers.

"Well, with that he's right," she said, laughing.

Belle glanced around at Zane with a puzzled look on her face.

He was so excited about meeting Dawn, he hoped his expression didn't seem wrong in the conversation. He was doing his best to contain his excitement.

"I was under the impression the institute was founded in 1880," Belle said.

"It was," Dawn said, smiling as she turned up Americana Boulevard and headed west out of the downtown area.

"Jesse and I will explain to both of you the structure of the institute after we're back on Warm Springs," Dawn said.

"That would be very helpful," Belle said. "So far, after only being here one morning, this seems far too good to be true, and you know what they say about things like that."

"I sure do," Dawn said. "And trust me, if I was in your spot, I would be questioning all the damn time. But I assure you, we have a lot of secrets, but not of the type that make this dangerous or sinister or anything else. And we're hoping to show you very quickly all those secrets."

"That would be nice," Zane said, laughing, pretending to go along. Somehow, he was controlling his excitement and just not blurting out something that would freak out Dawn and blow his cover.

But this was hard, really hard.

Dawn glanced back, smiling.

Then she turned to Belle. "I didn't say you were going to believe the secrets, however."

Belle glanced at Zane and then turned back to face forward and watch where they were headed.

Zane sat in the back seat as they climbed up and hill to what is called the First Bench, and Dawn made a left where the road split at the top of the hill.

Directly in front of them was a massive old cemetery shaded by huge old oak and pine and maple trees.

Again Belle glanced back at Zane with a puzzled look. Belle had not told Dawn where they were headed and Zane knew this wasn't the only old cemetery in the area.

Zane shook his head at Belle to tell her that he had not said anything. He honestly didn't know where they were heading either since Belle had not told him the name of the cemetery where her great, great grandfather was buried.

But, of course, Dawn would know where she buried her husband. Zane just hoped the slip of not asking which cemetery was purposeful.

Dawn turned into the first entrance to the cemetery, driving slowly between open wrought iron gates. A low rock wall ran along the road, dividing the cemetery from the busy street.

This cemetery, in its time, clearly must have been something, sitting up high overlooking the city below. Now the city had grown out and around it, so that the cemetery seemed to be almost in the downtown area.

Dawn drove carefully along what seemed like nothing more than a paved path through massive numbers of old tombstones and small monuments. They were clearly in the old section of the cemetery, and there were some large family name plots around.

Up ahead, Zane could see another big white Cadillac SUV parked off the small path of a road on the freshly mowed grass. As they approached, four others got out.

The only one Zane recognized was Director Parks.

"Seems we have company for our little excursion," Dawn said, laughing. "More founding members of the institute, if you will."

"You folks sure hold your age well," Zane said, trying to make a joke through being so stunned at what he was seeing.

Dawn laughed. "We do, don't we."

Dawn stopped behind the other SUV and shut off the car.

Zane had no idea at all what was happening. But he had no doubt that Belle was never going to believe what these five people were going to tell her.

Honestly, he didn't believe he was going to get a chance to meet these people, since one man, standing there in the cowboy hat, long duster coat, and cowboy boots was the famous Duster Kendal himself.

CHAPTER NINE

June 9th, 2020
Boise, Idaho

BELLE CRAWLED OUT and moved with Zane around the car to where the others were. She hadn't told anyone about where her great, great grandfather had been buried, but more than likely the fact that he was buried here had something to do with her special treatment.

She forced herself to take a deep breath of the slowly warming afternoon air that smelled of fresh-mowed grass. The huge old oak and pine trees in this section of the cemetery didn't let much of the sunlight through, so it felt cooler than she knew it actually was.

Everyone seemed to be about her age or just slightly older in looks, but there was something about the group that bothered Belle. She could not put her finger on it, but she felt she recognized a number of them.

One man wore a long dark duster even though the day was getting warmer by the minute, a dress shirt under the duster, jeans, cowboy boots, and a cowboy hat. He was the tallest.

He looked like he was right out of 1880.

The man beside him wore jeans, a light dress shirt, and tennis shoes. He was almost as tall as the other man and had short, dark hair. Belle thought he looked very, very familiar.

A woman stood beside the man in the coat. She was as tall as Zane and wore a silk blouse, dress jeans, and had her long hair pulled back as well. She smiled and seemed to radiate confidence with the smile.

"Belle, Zane," Director Parks said, "I would like you to meet Duster Kendal, Bonnie Kendal, and Madison."

Both Belle and Zane shook their hands as all three basically welcomed them.

Zane seemed almost shaking with nervousness, which surprised Belle. He didn't seem to be the type to have that sort of reaction. The guy could handle dangerous and emergency situations underground. Why was this making him nervous?

Duster was the man in the duster coat. Bonnie, the tall woman, was clearly his wife.

"We are very glad you decided to take us up on listening to an offer," Dawn said, turning to Belle. "We are glad you are here for a number of reasons, the most important being your genetics and genealogy research, of course."

Belle watched as all four of the others, including Director Parks, nodded in agreement.

"So Zane told Parks you came to see your great, great grandfather's grave," Dawn said. "So we figured we would take this time to start explaining some things that are difficult to believe about the institute to you."

Belle nodded, but said nothing. At this point, she figured it was just better to stay as calm and silent as possible to find out what was really happening.

"Let me show the grave to you," Dawn said, turning and leading the way off the road through the old tombstones across the freshly mowed grass. "It's been a while since I have been here, but I think I can find it."

Belle glanced at Zane who shook his head and just walked beside her. It felt good to have him there, even though he seemed in the dark as much as she was.

And he seemed to have recovered from his reaction meeting everyone. She would have to ask him about that later.

After about forty steps, with Belle and Zane following along followed by the other four, Dawn stopped and pointed to an old tombstone.

Belle watched her face as she suddenly seemed pained for a moment, then stepped back so that Belle and Zane and the others could see.

The stone was a double stone for a man and a woman, but the woman's side only had a name on it and nothing else.

On the man's side, it did not have a birth date on it. It simply read:

Madison Rogers
Died July 2nd, 1930
A great father. A great man.

The wife's name was Dawn Edwards Rogers. Nothing was filled out there.

Belle stared at it for a moment. She could feel the anger rising in her body, threatening to overwhelm her.

She turned to Dawn. "Is this some sort of game you are playing?"

Dawn shook her head. "No, this is just one of the secrets you promised to never reveal."

"And what secret exactly might that be?" Belle said, her voice low and cold and biting.

Damn she was mad. She just realized she had wasted a lot of money getting up here for this scam, whatever it was. And she was fairly certain she would never see that money repaid.

"My name is Dawn Edwards Rogers," Dawn said.

"I am supposed to be buried in that grave," Madison said, stepping forward. "But if you dug up that old casket, you would find it empty."

"So what kind of stupid vampire live-forever joke is going on here?" Belle asked.

The only two who didn't laugh at that were Belle and Zane. She didn't find it funny at all, but the other five sure did.

The laughing slowly died off among the tombstones and large ancient trees.

Belle was about to just walk off, get away from these nut cases who were claiming to be her great, great, grandparents, when Dawn pointed to Belle's tablet case.

"You connected with that?"

Belle nodded.

"Do a Google search on Dawn Edwards," Dawn said.

"That makes sense," Zane said.

Belle glanced at him as she pulled out her tablet, humoring the nut cases standing around her.

Zane stared at Dawn Edwards for a moment, then glanced at Madison Rogers for a moment before shaking his head. Belle had no idea what he had just realized.

Everyone stood, waiting, as Belle fired up her tablet and quickly typed in Dawn Edwards' name.

What came up first were the credentials for Dr. Dawn Edwards. And the instant she saw the name in that context, she remembered the books.

She was standing with Dawn Edwards, the bestselling historical author of a dozen books about the life and people in the Old West.

She glanced at Dawn, who just shrugged.

"Do a search on Madison Rogers," Director Parks said.

Belle quickly did, her hands shaking, because she knew exactly what she would find. He also was a bestselling author of over a dozen historical books, mostly about the mining wars and union fights in the Old West before 1900.

Belle had read all of their books and admired the intense reality of the details they brought to their work. But never once had it occurred to her to put their names with her great, great, grandparent's names.

Why would she?

After a moment of silence as they all stood among the tombstones, she looked up at Dawn again.

To one side, Zane's face was slightly pale as he must have realized without a search who was standing with them.

Dawn nodded and smiled, then stuck out her hand for the tablet. "May I show you a picture?"

Belle nodded and gave Dawn the tablet. Her anger was still there, but damned if it wasn't draining away slowly. She had found herself standing with two of the top researchers and bestsellers in her field in a cemetery. Anger didn't seem appropriate. She must have misunderstood what they were trying to say to her about the tombstone.

Dawn nodded and then motioned for Zane to look at the photo as well as she handed the tablet back to Belle.

Belle felt Zane move in beside her and look over her shoulder as she looked at a picture of four people taken on a rough board sidewalk of an old mining town.

"I wrote a number of my books about the lost mining town of Roosevelt, Idaho," Dawn said.

Belle nodded, noting the date hand-written on the old photo. "That's some great Photoshop work," Belle said.

"It's a real, documented picture, Dawn said. "taken on the date shown on the picture by Anderson James, the great western photographer. It has never been doctored."

"You showing them the picture that got me into this craziness," Parks asked.

Dawn laughed. "I figured it would be as good a one as any."

"Now I know how they are feeling," Director Parks said. "The woman in that picture is Dr. Kelli Rae. First time she recognized me in a picture like that, I was damn angry, let me tell you."

Belle was stunned as she looked at the picture of Duster Kendal, Madison Rogers, Parks, and yet another bestselling historical researcher, Dr. Kelli Rae in an impossible picture.

"I'm not sure what I'm feeling," Belle said. "Disappointment, mostly, because I was hoping to work here for the summer on my research."

"I must admit," Zane said, "you five sound like a bunch of nut cases."

Belle was stunned that all five just laughed.

"We don't blame you at all for feeling that way," Dawn said after a moment. "In fact, we always expect it of a new researcher. But can we ask you one favor? Just come back to the institute with us and let us show you exactly what is happening. And how that picture can exist in history."

Belle looked at Zane, who now seemed to be under control.

After a moment, he took a deep breath and glanced at her and nodded.

"If Zane goes along, I'll go," she said.

"Thank you," Dawn said.

At that, all five of the others turned back toward the cars.

"I'm sorry," Zane whispered to Belle.

"Let's hear them out and then figure out what to do," Belle said.

"I agree," Zane said, nodding.

She glanced down at the gravestone, then up at the people walking back toward the cars. Two of the most popular and best historical writers of all time were in the group. Of that, there was no doubt.

But why would those two writers want her to believe she was their great, great, granddaughter? What point would doing that win?

Belle pointed to the old gravestone, clearly weathered, then looked at Zane. "Want to explain to me why they pulled that scam?"

"Not a clue," he said, shaking his head. "Not one damn clue. You want to turn and head the other direction?"

"A large part of me says we should," Belle said, glancing at Zane. "But let's hear them out. If we don't, we will always ask ourselves what this was all about."

"Good point," Zane said, nodding. "We stick together."

"I like the sound of that," Belle said, trying to smile at him.

But honestly, at the moment, she didn't feel much like smiling.

CHAPTER TEN

June 9th, 2020
Boise, Idaho

ZANE WAS GLAD that the first Cadillac had already left by the time he and Belle wound back through the old tombstones to the SUV. It was everything he could do to try to keep his cover, but all along it was clear the founding members were not talking to him. Their focus

was on Belle completely. So more than likely, his cover was blown with them.

So the best thing he could do was just go along and help Belle through the shock of what was about to come.

He just hoped he had reacted as she had expected. If he blew his cover too fast with her, they would all lose her, and he didn't want to do that. He wanted to get to know her a lot, lot more.

"Sorry to shock you like this," Dawn said as she opened the doors and then moved around to the driver's side. "We have learned over the years this is the best way."

"We thought about heading in the other direction," Belle said as they all three climbed into the big SUV and Dawn got the car started and the air-conditioning going. The afternoon was slowly growing warm and promised to be even warmer before the cool night air took over again.

"I would not have blamed you in the slightest," Dawn said. "But after we show you some things and you hear us out, I think you'll be glad you stayed. But at any point you have the option of leaving. You just have to abide by the nondisclosure agreement is all we ask."

Zane was about to say something snide about who would believe he met a bunch of crazy people, but decided not to. No point in pushing his cover too far.

As Dawn pulled the big SUV off the grass and back onto the path of a road that wound under the trees through the old tombstones, she said, "Better do a Google search on Duster and Bonnie Kendal as well, so you know who they are."

Belle nodded and pulled out her tablet again.

Zane decided it was just better to sit in the back seat and say nothing. He needed to be very careful and not just assume that since they weren't talking at him they knew when he was from.

From the front seat, as Dawn took the big SUV out of the cemetery and back into traffic, Belle said, "Oh, my."

She looked at Dawn, then back at the tablet.

"Duster and Bonnie have funded a couple hundred mathematics scholarships in ten different major universities," Dawn said. "And at MIT and Cal Tech they have buildings named after them. They have more money than they seem to be able to give away. All fourteen of the founding members are now fantastically rich, which is why the institute can do what it does for historical researchers."

Well, that answered part of that question for Belle, but only a slight part. Zane was glad Dawn had tried to clear that quickly.

Zane watched as Belle just shook her head, then quickly passed the tablet back to him.

From the page Belle had pulled up, it showed that Bonnie and Duster Kendal were acclaimed mathematicians doing work on alternate timelines. Both of them had more high-level degrees in mathematics than he and Belle put together in history.

Zane already knew that and so much more about them. That was why he had been so excited to actually meet them. He was just damn lucky to have not fainted dead away. That would have been embarrassing.

"Wow," Zane said, handing the tablet back to Belle. "So four of the five of you *founding members* have impressive credentials."

"Actually," Dawn said, "all fourteen total founding members have major credentials in their fields, including Director Parks."

"But the institute has been around since 1880," Belle said. "I researched it as much as I could before wasting my money coming up here."

Dawn nodded. "It has been. And that's the contradiction we hope to explain to you."

"And that picture," Zane said. "How it can be a fake and yet not be a fake to you?"

Dawn laughed and nodded. "It's not a fake, but when Parks was in your position," glancing at Belle, "back right before we started the institute three years ago, he had the same reaction and wanted to know the same thing. And wow was he angry. You do not want to see him angry."

"So how come I am just now being told all this after nine months?" Zane asked.

Dawn pointed at Belle. "The reality of this information is easier to grasp with two people at the same time. Belle has been the first person to join the researchers at the institute since you joined that we feel is ready for the information we want to show you. And besides, we really need your caving skills for a project down the road."

Zane sort of felt surprised at that. Why would the institute need his caving skills? That made no sense at all.

"Why is that?" Belle asked. "What was he doing that made him interesting to you over all the others here doing research, besides his skills at surviving in caves and being a damn fine writer?"

Zane smiled at that. And her question hit right at a critical factor in all institute decisions on who came on board and who didn't.

Dawn laughed. "As you also have, Belle, Zane has a laser intensity on his research and a drive to make every detail in his books as accurate as he possibly can. His passion for historical research on his chosen topic equals yours and the rest of the historical researchers who know the reality of the institute."

"Doesn't every historical writer have that kind of intensity?" Zane asked, feeling complimented while giving Dawn the chance to explain more.

"No," Dawn said, shaking her head. "We have let almost a dozen researchers into the institute at the entry level you have been at over the last few months, Zane. You have met many of them, and you are the only one. A number have left already, the others will in time, without ever knowing what we are about to show you two."

"But you know nothing about me," Belle said. "I have not been tested."

Dawn again smiled. "We have been waiting for you to come through our front door. If you had not agreed to listen to our offer by the end of the summer, we would have gone and recruited you in August."

"I was vetted?" Belle asked, staring at Dawn.

Zane could not tell if Belle was angry at that, or accepting the fact.

"You both were," Dawn said, nodding. "We saw both of you coming before either of you got here. Parks also owns a private detective agency and part of his agency's job is to vet and do background checks on all historical researchers working and coming into the field."

Dawn laughed. "Let me tell you a quick story. Before the institute, before he knew what we are about to show you, Jesse, Director Parks, was doing a background check for Bonnie and Duster on Dr. Kelli Rae. She caught him, which let me tell you, is almost impossible.

She caught him because of that picture I showed you."

Dawn shook her head, smiling for some reason at the memory. Then she went on with her story as she deftly got them through the downtown Boise traffic.

"Kelli has a memory for faces and when she saw Jesse in the picture, then in real life, she thought she was seeing a ghost, or a distant relative. She knew the picture was real since she knew the photographer's work and had gotten the picture from the historical society the year before."

"So what happened?" Belle asked as Dawn turned the big SUV onto Warm Springs Avenue and headed away from town toward the institute.

Dawn laughed. "Both Jesse and Kelli were even angrier than you are when Bonnie and Duster and Madison and I met with them. They allowed us to show them what actually was going on, as you are allowing us. And it was Jesse who came up with the idea for the institute the very next day."

Suddenly Belle glanced back at Zane, her eyes wide.

Then she looked at Dawn again. "You ever heard of the term *Angel of San Francisco*?"

Dawn smiled and nodded.

"I've seen pictures of the *Angel of San Francisco*," Belle said. "A couple of them are actually hanging in the historical department at Stanford."

Dawn again just smiled.

"Oh, shit," Belle said, shaking her head and turning back to face forward as they got closer to the institute.

"You want to clue me in on who this *Angel of San Francisco* is?" Zane asked. "My research sort of keeps me focused underground, if you know what I mean."

Dawn laughed.

Belle turned in her seat to look at Zane.

Zane was stunned. Belle's eyes looked almost haunted.

"From about 1890 through the big San Francisco earthquake and up to about 1930," Belle said, "the *Angel of San Francisco* saved and helped more people than can be counted. She never once asked for a favor in return and she did what she did without any fanfare. There are only a few dozen pictures of her that have survived down through time."

Belle pulled the big SUV into the institute driveway.

"Okay, so?" Zane asked.

"Her real name was Bonnie Kendal," Belle said. "And I now recognize her from the pictures in my department in Stanford."

With that, Belle just turned around and faced forward as Dawn took the big Cadillac to the parking area in the back.

Zane had no idea at all what to say. It looked like Belle was starting to slowly understand.

And that would help her very shortly.

CHAPTER ELEVEN

June 9th, 2020
Boise, Idaho

THE AFTERNOON AIR had warmed up, even under the big overhanging willow trees that shaded part of the parking area behind the big institute building. Zane could hear only the sounds of the river below the estate as he slowly climbed out.

The other SUV was already there and no one was around.

So he joined Belle and followed Dawn toward the back door that went into a basement under the wrap-around back porch on the big mansion. He had sat on that porch many afternoons, sipping on a Diet Coke before going back in to work, or heading down the path toward his apartment.

That porch had a wonderful view, past the large garage building and through the trees and out over the slowly flowing river. He had been told that in the summer thousands of people floating in tubes and small rafts floated by, but it was still too early in the summer and the water was moving too fast for that.

He had been looking forward to seeing that and maybe floating the river one afternoon.

Dawn led them in the back door and across the basement full of old history books toward the staircase that led upstairs. The floor was covered with a thin carpet and the shelves were made of older wood. It felt like this room had been a fruit cellar before the institute fitted it with books that were seldom used.

Of course, he knew that wasn't the case. This had always been a decoy room right from the start in 1880.

He had spent a few hours down here browsing in these old books, but had found nothing interesting in the slightest.

Dawn glanced up the stairs, then back to make sure the door outside was closed, then she stepped past the stairs into an alcove of books and touched a side of one shelf.

"Welcome Dr. Edwards," a female voice said.

Goldie. Zane wasn't surprised to hear the same voice that was in the apartments.

A shelf unit slid back silently and Dawn indicated that he and Belle should follow her into a well-lit corridor beyond.

As he stepped into the corridor, the wall of books behind them slid closed with a click.

"Can we get out of here now?" Belle asked.

She clearly did not like the feeling of being trapped with a bunch of nut cases.

"Sure," Dawn said. "Goldie will open the door for you if no one is outside in the small library."

Zane nodded to Belle who only smiled faintly. Then he followed Dawn and Belle into what looked like a massive computer room. The room was the size of a small grocery store and had aisles and aisles of what looked like very expensive servers. None of them seemed to be working at all, none of their lights were blinking, and the big room was dead silent and a little cool.

Dawn walked over to one wall without explaining the room and touched a screen.

"This brings up a map of the entire facility," Dawn said. "We're the three dots here."

Again Zane was impressed at the security feature that hinted at. It was far advanced for this time. Same level as his time period.

Dawn pointed to three dots against one wall in the very center of a huge, sprawling map that showed that this underground area was far, far bigger than just the institute building above it.

"The mansions on both sides are owned by the institute," Dawn said. "The underground secret part stretches under all three and goes into the ground three levels deep. I'll explain later what some of the areas are for, and why three buildings."

Zane was flat impressed that Dawn was saying as much as she was. In his time, a hundred years in the future, the third building, the building for future time travelers beyond his time, wasn't even mentioned.

Belle just stood staring at the screen and shaking her head.

"Wow," she said. "How many people work down here?"

"There are only thirty people counting you two who know about this place at this point in time," Dawn said.

"So why so much room?" Belle asked.

"Because we hope to continue to expand slowly into the future the work being done here," Dawn said. "Right from the start this was built for the future."

"The three years ago start or the 1880 start?" Zane asked.

"Yes," Dawn said, smiling.

Zane just shook his head and Belle looked annoyed, so he said what he knew Belle was thinking. "At some point a straight answer is going to be needed."

"That was a straight answer," Dawn said, moving the image on the screen to the next level down. Four dots appeared there just below them, from what Zane could tell.

"Good," Dawn said. "They are in a room we call the living room."

Zane loved the living room. He had spent many a wonderful hour in that big cavern room in the future, talking with other researchers. And since it was mostly just a large cave, he felt completely at home.

Then Dawn pointed to numbers of areas on the screen. "These screens are everywhere in this place and the exits are marked. Goldie will only let you out if there is no one on the other side. So sometimes you might have to try a second exit."

With that, Dawn headed down one row of the big servers.

"What are all these for?" Belle asked, indicating the servers.

"At times Bonnie and Duster and the other four mathematicians that are involved in all this need massive computing power," Dawn said. "My understanding is that all this is extra power for those major math problems. There are ten rooms bigger than this at different points on the three levels."

"These are mostly servers," Zane said. "More than likely this room is just storage."

He knew for a fact that in the future this room would be used for Belle's genetics project storage in far more modern equipment, but he didn't say that.

Dawn nodded. "Makes sense. I never honestly asked anyone."

She went through a fire door and down a staircase carved out of rock. Their footsteps echoed in the stairwell.

"There is an elevator under each building that also goes up into a hidden room in the mansions above, but most of us find it easier to just take the stairs when moving around down here."

Zane nodded. It was that way a hundred years in the future as well.

The staircase did two switchbacks before Dawn went through another metal fire door and out into a very high-ceiling room.

It was clear the room was a cavern and had been carved out of the bedrock. Zane would have loved to have been part of the massive construction project on this place in 1880. From what he understood from institute history, the founders had brought in crews from major eastern cities, housed them away from the locals, and then rotated them out regularly so no one crew would know the extent of everything.

The room they had entered called the Living Room was larger than most high

school gyms and was set up like a giant living room on steroids.

A good dozen couch-and-chair areas were scattered around a massive stone fireplace that clearly burnt real wood from the faint odor of wood fire that seemed to fill the place. All the couches and chairs were brown cloth covered and overstuffed. Each area had maple end tables and a large coffee table in front of the couch.

Tall fake trees of some sort or another divided the areas, giving each a sense of privacy.

Across from the massive lounge area was a modern kitchen with a brown granite counter that seemed to stretch longer than many bars in old fashion saloons. Twenty or so bar stools were on the lounge side of the counter and on the other side was a duplicate kitchen, with two modern stainless fridges, two stoves, three large sinks, and more dark-stained cabinets than Zane could imagine in five normal kitchens.

The institute founders never thought small in the construction of this place, and this room showed that. Zane's favorite place a hundred years in the future was over near the fireplace.

But without a lot of people coming and going, this cavern just felt empty.

Director Parks, Madison, Duster, and Bonnie all were at one end of the kitchen counter. Bonnie was doing something on the kitchen side while the three men sat at the counter with drinks of some sort in front of them.

Zane again hesitated. He couldn't believe he was actually talking with some of the founders. Especially Bonnie and Duster. He needed to be extra, extra careful with what he said.

"Let's move over to the couches," Dawn said as they approached the group.

"Need something to drink?" Bonnie asked them.

"Bottle of water would be nice," Dawn said, indicating a group of couches close to the kitchen area.

Zane agreed that water would be good, as did Belle.

Then making sure he stayed close to Belle, they went over and sat down on the closest couch.

The other five sat in the chairs across from them after Bonnie brought three plastic bottles of cold water.

No one said a word and Zane could feel the tension in the air.

And if this group had any chance at all of getting Belle to stay until dinner, they had a lot of explaining to do to her, and quickly.

A whole hell of a lot.

And they didn't know it, but a lot of the future of the institute rode on this coming conversation with her.

CHAPTER TWELVE

June 9th, 2020
Boise, Idaho

SO FAR THIS day had been one stunning thing after another for Belle.

From the offer to join the researchers at the institute, to the knowledge that there was a wonderful apartment for her to live in and free food.

And she had met a man she had been instantly attracted to, someone she could think of as an equal. Someone who shared her same passions and interests.

Then the day had seemed to just go sideways and she was having a very difficult time trying to let her mind catch up. Two of the great historical researchers working today, two people she almost idolized for their work, had basically said they were her great, great, grandparents.

And now this incredible underground area.

Nothing was making sense.

Beside her, Zane was clearly worried and tense as well.

They both needed answers and they needed them soon.

Bonnie glanced around and then looked directly at Belle with her intense dark eyes. She seemed to be in control and calm, something that Belle didn't understand completely in this situation.

"I'm going to give you a very short story about how all this came about," Bonnie said. "You will not believe me, remember that. But after the short story, we would ask that you trust us just long enough to allow us to show you one more thing."

Belle nodded.

Beside her Zane made no movement at all.

"Back in the 1870s, Duster's family had a gold mine that ran out of gold fairly quickly," Bonnie said. "The mine was closed and handed down through the years until Duster's father showed it to the two of us."

Bonnie took a sip of water and sat the bottle on the end table beside her chair.

"At one point," Bonnie said, "Duster's grandfather had decided to try to work the mine and had opened it back up and broke into a massive room of crystals. A cavern that is almost impossible to imagine even when you see it. The discovery scared him and he closed it up, showed it to Duster's dad, who only maintained the mine and never told anyone. When he showed it to us, we both had the idea of

what the giant cavern was. But it took us three years of intense research and calculations to prove our theory correct."

Belle just kept listening.

"You know that Duster and I have advanced degrees in theoretical mathematics?" Bonnie asked.

"Dawn had us do a search for your names on the way back here," Belle said.

Bonnie nodded thanks to Dawn.

"In simple terms, a major theory of physics now is that matter, energy, and time are all connected in fashions we do not yet understand," Bonnie said. "Our calculations always came to the conclusion that there was a physical location where all three needed to manifest in a physical form. Until the big cavern in the mine, we assumed that was only in theory."

"Are you saying that physical location exists in a mine?" Belle asked. She was following, but barely.

"I am," Bonnie said, "but let me finish."

Zane nodded and Belle sat back.

Belle wanted to reach over and put her hand on his, but didn't. They both needed to concentrate right now, but holding his hand would most certainly calm her some.

Bonnie went on. "When any person makes any decision at all, math proves that timelines split from that decision. For example, you decided to hear us out and are sitting here in billions of timelines. There are billions of timelines in which you decided to walk away in the cemetery."

Belle shook her head. "You mean a timeline splits because of what I picked for lunch? That seems ludicrous."

"Math proves it without a doubt," Bonnie said. "But most split timelines merge back into one another if the changes don't have any impact. Time and energy and matter are fluid. But using your example, for lunch you picked one food and were fine, but in billions of other timelines you picked another food that was tainted and you got sick and by being sick, missed something important and the timelines stayed apart."

"That would mean there are almost an infinite number of timelines," Zane said.

"That is correct," Bonnie said. "The cavern we found merges with untold numbers of other caverns with billions of crystals on the walls in every cavern. We believe the crystals in the first cavern are the ones that are closest to this timeline we sit in."

"It must be one damn big cavern," Zane said.

"The Superdome in New Orleans would fit inside just the first cavern without touching the walls or the ceiling," Bonnie said flatly. "And every inch of it is covered by crystals of various sizes and every crystal represents a timeline almost identical in all aspects to this timeline we sit in now."

Zane sat back hard, clearly stunned at the idea of a cavern that large.

Belle just shook her head. "I'm not imagining something that big, so go on and explain how this concerns us."

Bonnie nodded. "After Duster and I had all the math together, we figured out a way to step into other timelines from this timeline, into the past of other timelines. Effectively, time traveling into the past."

Belle shook her head and was about to get up and ask for the closest exit.

"I think it's time we show them a few of the crystals from the cavern," Duster said, standing. "Then give them time to come up with questions over some

afternoon snacks, or have them head for the door."

Bonnie nodded and looked directly at Belle. "Just give us fifteen more minutes of your time. Please?"

"Yes, please," Director Parks said.

Belle glanced at Zane who nodded and then said, "Why not?"

He stood.

"Fifteen minutes," Belle said, standing beside him as everyone stood. "Then I'm booking a plane back to San Francisco."

"And I'm going with her," Zane said.

Duster nodded and turned and started off toward a door off to one side of the large kitchen area.

Bonnie and Madison followed.

Dawn looked at Belle and Zane. "I told you that you would not believe us, but let us at least show you one more thing before you rightfully walk away."

"I'll be honest," Belle said, looking at Dawn. "If I didn't respect you and Madison's work so much, I would have already been gone."

"Thank you," Dawn said, nodding slightly in appreciation. She then turned and followed the others leaving Belle and Zane to follow behind.

CHAPTER THIRTEEN

June 9th, 2020
Boise, Idaho

ZANE HAD BEEN surprised that Belle was willing to give these people any more time, let alone trust them to take them deeper underground. She had some real courage, he had to give her that.

He just wasn't sure how to play all this. He needed to remain in part, as if from this time. But he honestly hated to lie to anyone, especially Belle.

He and Belle followed the five down even deeper into the underground cavern under the old institute building. The deeper they went, the more concerned he could tell that Belle was getting. And he honestly didn't blame her in the slightest.

Plus, this area they were headed was an area he hadn't been in before.

On the third level down, Duster led the group through another door and into a large storage area full of massive amounts of supplies, vintage clothing hanging on racks, and older model guns and ammunition behind locked doors.

It was like a Walmart of old western clothes and supplies.

There had to be fifty long wooden tables in the large cavern, all with lights hanging from the ceiling down over the tables.

Zane found this really impressive. The supply area for his travel time was for this time and forward. This supply area was for 1880 forward. Wow, what a difference.

He knew that the institute worked like a giant train station with master stop areas. From one hundred years in the future, he had come back as far as he could, to what everyone called the First Step. He lived in the time of the Second Step and there were areas of the institute that he knew were Third Step and maybe even Fourth Step. No one in Step Two talked of them.

The private step areas in the institute kept the time travelers from different centuries from going back too far at once. Like a train station, you had to change areas to keep stepping back into the past.

Duster and the rest just walked through the warehouse without a word of explanation to Belle.

Zane glanced at Belle who, for the first time, was looking a little panicked. She clearly was thinking that there was no reason for this vast warehouse of vintage clothing and supplies if what they were saying about time travel wasn't actually true.

On the other side of the storage cavern was a wall of about thirty doors spaced evenly along the carved-stone wall like hotel room doors. Duster went through the door closest to the right wall of the supply area and into a long room.

The room wasn't more than a normal living room wide, but it must have been the length of a football field long, if not longer, carved out of the solid rock.

Wooden tables stretched along the length of the center of the room with a simple wooden box on each table.

A wire fence that went from floor to ceiling ran along both walls on both sides of the room, making the room look like it had a fenced in hallway down the middle.

And through the fence Zane could see thousands and thousands of slots carved into the rock. Each slot held a glowing pink crystal.

Zane knew that each crystal had been brought to the institute from the original cavern and basically represented a timeline.

Wires ran from each box on each table and through the fence. All the wires were on the ground.

Each crystal was clearly marked on the wall under its slot with a lined ledger. Some ledgers had notations on them, others were blank.

"Oh, shit," Belle said softly.

Zane said nothing. He was feeling stunned being in this area. From here, he could go all the way back to the start of the institute in 1880 if he wanted. The very idea of that scared him more than he wanted to admit.

"We want to show you what exactly we are talking about," Bonnie said to Belle.

Duster moved over and opened up a gate in the fence near the closest machine, then he put on thick leather gloves and hooked up two wires to one of the crystals.

"Never touch a crystal with your bare hands," Duster said to Belle as he came back out of the fence-protected area and shut the gate. "Extreme energy. More than we've been able to calculate so far at least."

Zane could only nod. Even in his time the scientists working at the institute had not been able to calculate the energy coming from a crystal.

Duster turned to Director Parks. "Jesse, you mind staying behind for the two minutes as an example?"

"Glad to," Director Parks said, smiling.

With the leather gloves still on, Duster adjusted a fairly plain looking dial on one side of the wooden box, then hooked up both wires and took off the gloves.

Zane was amazed that even a hundred years into the future, this was still exactly the same system every traveler used.

"Move in close to the wooden box," Bonnie said as Dawn and Madison and Duster did.

"Trust me," Dawn said to Belle, "this will not hurt and if you want to really understand what is happening here, this is the easiest way."

Zane was totally numb at this point. He couldn't believe he was making a second step jump, but he moved to the box with Belle.

The two of them were now between Dawn and Bonnie.

"On the count of three, just touch the wooden box at the same time," Bonnie said.

Director Parks moved around so that he was standing just across the table from Zane and Belle.

"One, two, three," Bonnie said.

Zane touched the wooden box at the same time as the rest of them.

Nothing happened at all, or at least that was what it always felt like.

Except that Director Parks just vanished without a trace.

Or a sound.

"Where did Director Parks go?" Belle asked, her voice sounding almost panicked as all six of them stepped back from the box.

"He didn't go anywhere," Dawn said. "We did. We are now in the timeline that is represented by that crystal there on the wall. In December of 1885."

She pointed to the crystal and Zane just shook his head. He had made a second step jump. How fantastic!

"Some illusion," Belle said.

Duster turned to Bonnie. "You want to wait here and pull the plug in twenty minutes, save us the walk back down here?"

"Glad to," Bonnie said, smiling.

"If you think that was an illusion," Duster said, glancing at Belle before turning and heading back the way they had come, "let me show you a real doozy."

"I can only wait," Belle said.

Zane was having trouble not jumping up and down with excitement and blowing his cover. He had done what few travelers in his time had ever done. He had made a Second Step jump back in time. He was now over two hundred and thirty-five years back in history from his own time.

Wow, just wow.

CHAPTER FOURTEEN

June 9th, 2020
Boise, Idaho

BELLE STAYED BESIDE Zane as they followed Duster and Dawn and Madison out of the fenced crystal room and through the warehouse of old clothes and supplies. The room did not look as full as when they had gone through a few minutes ago.

That fact alone bothered her more than she wanted to think about. And Director Parks just vanishing right in front of her eyes seemed flat impossible.

Zane seemed to be handling this a lot better than she was. He seemed almost excited, but was containing it. But she could feel it from him.

She wasn't letting herself believe they had actually traveled in time. But at the moment she had no idea at all what was happening.

They all got into the elevator that looked like an antique.

"This isn't as old as it looks," Dawn said, indicating the elevator. "We just had to camouflage it in case someone who wasn't supposed to be in here got in."

The ride up three floors was quick and the elevator emptied them into a wide room with no furnishings at all. Just polished pine floors, painted walls, and two doors.

"That goes into the back part of the institute," Dawn said, pointing to one door. "This one goes into the main room."

"There's no door into that main room," Belle said.

"Lots of secrets around here," Dawn said, laughing.

Duster looked through what seemed to be some sort of viewfinder, then turned to them. "This will tell you if anyone who doesn't belong is in the main room. As expected, no one at all is there."

He pushed the door open slowly and led the way into the main room of the institute, the one where just this morning she had met Zane.

His big desk was there, only with no computers on it. A fire was crackling softly in the fireplace, and the same furniture sat in front of the fireplace. Even the drapes on the windows were the same and were pulled.

The room had a slight chill to it as well.

Belle glanced around as she stepped into the big room and the door slid closed with a click.

It now looked exactly like a wall with a large framed picture on it. No way to ever tell there was a door there.

"Now that's impressive," Belle said. "You would never know there was a door there."

"Good," Duster said. "Latch to open it is built into the trim on the column there beside the door."

He pointed to it and Belle nodded.

Zane had known it was there, but he played along as if he hadn't.

"Now let's take a look outside," Duster said, turning toward the front door.

"I'm staying right here," Dawn said.

"Wimp," Madison said, laughing.

Duster opened the big front door and stepped outside into the gray light beyond the door.

Belle felt the incredible cold hit her almost instantly as she and Zane moved toward the front door.

Duster and Madison both moved out onto the front porch and Zane and Belle followed. Behind them Dawn pushed the big front door closed.

Belle was having a very hard time grasping what she was seeing and feeling.

A light snow was blowing through the trees in front of the mansion. The leaves were long gone from the big trees, and it had to be twenty degrees, if that.

The cold cut through her thin shirt like it wasn't there. Now she wished she had kept on her sweatshirt, but she doubted it would have helped that much.

Through the snow she could see the stone wall along the front of the mansion, but it had no hedge growing on it.

And the Warm Springs Avenue she could see beyond the wall wasn't anything more than a wagon trail.

"Welcome to December 17th, 1885," Duster said. "It's about two in the afternoon."

"Amazing" Zane asked, moving toward the front of the porch.

"How is this possible?" Belle asked.

"We stepped into another timeline," Duster said. "One that is for every intent and purpose identical to our timeline."

"So you were telling us the truth?" Belle asked.

"We were," Duster said. "Every word. And we have a lot more to explain, but you would not have stood for it without seeing and experiencing this first."

Belle was starting to shake from the cold, but she turned to Madison. "So you really are my great, great, grandfather?"

"Actually, the me from another timeline," Madison said. "We can't travel back in our own timeline. But yes, I am and genetics will prove it to you as well."

"Mind of I walk out to the road?" Zane asked.

Duster laughed. "Be my guest."

Zane stepped carefully down the snow-covered front steps of the mansion and started out toward the front gate.

"I need to see this as well," Belle said.

"We'll be inside," Duster said.

"Zane, wait," Belle shouted through the light snow.

Zane turned around as she carefully went down the snow-covered front stairs and followed him. She was so cold, she could barely feel her arms and feet, but that didn't matter at the moment. She needed to prove to herself as well this was actually happening.

He took her hand as she got closer and she wished she could feel it.

Then the two of them walked toward the front gate of the institute together, not saying a word.

Zane managed to get the wrought iron gate open and they walked into the middle of the wagon road that went past the mansion.

Belle flat could not believe what she was seeing and feeling.

Clearly she was in the past.

And at a different time of the year as well.

The two mansions on either side of the main institute building were all that was here. No sign at all of anything else being built along this wagon road.

"They were telling us the truth," Zane said simply. "We are standing in 1885."

"They are offering us this so we can research our books better," Belle said. "No wonder Dawn and Madison's books have such crisp details."

If she wasn't so cold, she would be jumping up and down with excitement.

The impossible really was possible.

Zane looked both directions down the wagon road, then back at the institute buildings over the wall.

Then he let go of her hand and put his arm around her shoulder. "I've seen enough. How about you?"

She was so cold that all she could do was nod. The Stanford area got cold in the winter, but nothing like this.

"Let's head back," he said.

They had made it back through the gate and were about halfway to the front porch, both of them staggering from the intense cold, when suddenly they found themselves touching the wooden box in the long crystal room three levels underground.

Bonnie had a wire in a gloved hand and was smiling at them. Director Parks was basically standing in the same place he had been.

Bonnie, Duster, Madison, and Dawn were also touching the box.

Belle's legs almost collapsed under her, but she caught herself on the table. She was shivering and wet and colder than she had ever remembered being before.

Dawn got on one side of her and Bonnie on the other and Madison moved to help Zane.

"Let's get you both to a hot shower, dry clothes, and some hot chocolate," Bonnie said as they headed for the door of the crystal room. "Then over some early dinner we can explain all this in more detail."

All Belle could do was nod, but she had to admit, that sounded wonderful.

Especially the hot shower part.

PART TWO
The Mission

CHAPTER FIFTEEN

June 9th, 2020
Boise, Idaho

BELLE FELT ALMOST warm again after the shower and getting into the sweatpants and sweatshirt that Dawn had gotten for her. Those and the warm slippers and she felt almost human. She and Zane had only been out in the cold for ten minutes, and both of them had been dressed for a warm summer's day, not a December snowstorm.

Zane had already arrived back into the massive cavern they called the Living Room and was standing beside the long counter sipping on a cup of wonderful-smelling hot chocolate. Dawn was standing near one end of the counter and Bonnie and Duster were behind the counter near the fridge. Parks and Madison were nowhere to be seen.

Dawn smiled at her and slid Belle a cup of the same hot chocolate.

Then the five of them again moved to the closest couch and chair grouping.

Zane was also in sweatpants and a sweatshirt that had a Boise State logo on it. He looked even better than he had before, if that was possible. He sat next to her on the couch facing the other three.

She was so glad he was with her on this. She couldn't imagine going through this alone, even though she had only known Zane for a few hours today. It felt much longer for some reason.

It felt odd to Belle that even though Dawn and Bonnie and Duster were about her age, they felt much, much older. That also was a strange feeling, and she had a hunch she was about to find out why it existed.

Belle let herself sip on the hot chocolate for a second, letting the warmth and wonderful sweet taste clear her mind even more from the shower. Then she looked up at Dawn.

"So we can travel in time," Belle said.

Dawn nodded.

"And you have used that to get the fantastic sense of reality and details in your books," Belle said.

Dawn nodded. "So explain to me a little more about how this works, and then why you showed me all this."

Zane was saying nothing, just letting Dawn go, and nodding. She had no idea what he was thinking at the moment.

Dawn glanced at Bonnie and Duster and both nodded that she should go ahead.

"Bonnie and Duster discovered that the crystals in a vast cavern are all the physical representations of other alternate timelines," Dawn said. "We are inside one such crystal now. Time and energy and matter are all connected and on the matter side, the crystals are the representation."

"I won't pretend to understand the math or physics on that," Belle said. "So before I get confused, keep going in general."

Dawn smiled and went on. "When those wires are hooked up to that wooden box and the device in the box, anyone touching that box can go to the other timeline for two minutes and fifteen seconds."

Belle shook her head. "We were in the past for at least twenty minutes, weren't we?"

"We were," Dawn said. "And in that timeline, we lived those twenty minutes. But in this timeline, only two minutes and fifteen seconds passed."

Belle shook her head, suddenly understanding how Dawn and Madison could claim to be her great, great, grandparents.

"So you can go to another timeline, live for decades and decades, and then return and only two minutes will have passed?" Belle asked.

"Exactly," Dawn said. "And if you die in another timeline, you end up back in your own timeline perfectly alive and fine."

"Does the timeline you go to and live in sort of reset when you vanish?" Belle asked.

"No," Dawn said. "You are evidence of that."

Belle decided to let that slide for the moment.

Zane was saying nothing, mostly just nodding and listening and sipping his hot chocolate. And she wasn't sure why. But she was still very glad he was beside her.

"When we went back to the 1885 in December," Bonnie said, "we started a new timeline, a new crystal somewhere in the cavern. Since we changed nothing while there, that timeline got absorbed, for lack of a better way of putting it, back into the regular timelines."

Belle sipped on her hot chocolate and looked around at the huge cavern two levels under the fantastic mansion on Warm Springs Avenue. "It seems that my worry about funding of the institute no longer matters."

Dawn smiled. "Being able to travel back in time and understand what is going to happen allows a person to get very rich."

"We started making investments in different timelines back in the 1880s," Duster said. "Money is no longer an issue nor will it ever be for any of us, you included."

Belle was having a hard time still believing all this, but she now understood enough to need a few more answers.

"So why me? And why Zane?"

Dawn nodded to Duster who sat forward. "Dr. Russell, we hope that you will join the institute and build us, over time, the most extensive data bank of genealogy records backed up by genetics. And do it for every human in history and in all timelines."

Belle laughed, flat shocked at the idea. "That's a dream job for me, I must agree. But that would take hundreds of years, if that. And computer and data storage needed for that size project is beyond anything we have at this moment in time."

Belle couldn't let herself believe that was possible. She could almost accept traveling in time easier than that job.

Bonnie looked at her with an intent look. "Time and technology are not an issue."

"Can I ask how long you have all lived?" Zane asked, sitting forward suddenly as Belle tried to grasp what Bonnie had said enough to even form a question.

Bonnie and Duster both shrugged. "I stopped counting when we had lived past a thousand years," Bonnie said.

"And that was a long time ago," Duster said.

"I'm still counting," Dawn said, "because I know we get this question from

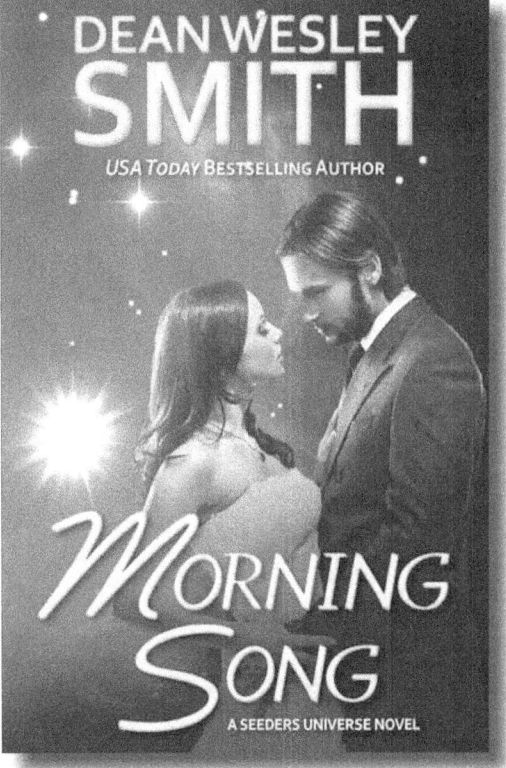

anyone coming into the institute at this level. Madison and I have lived now for about six thousand years in various time-lines."

"Holy shit," Zane said, sitting back.

Belle flat didn't know what to feel. Everything in her body felt numb.

Bonnie looked at Belle. "As I said, Dr. Russell, time is not an issue for you any-more. Money is not an issue. And technology is not an issue. The only question is would you like to tackle such a massive project?"

"Let me think about that for a moment," Belle said, doing her best to catch her breath and just calm her mind.

But deep down she knew the answer instantly. Of course she would.

"How about me?" Zane asked.

Duster looked at Zane and smiled. "Dr. Thomas, or should I say Dr. Logan, we would like your help in a massive underground exploration project."

Zane snapped back as if hit.

Belle glanced at him as he set his hot chocolate mug on the coffee table. His hand was shaking.

What had just happened?

"You knew?" Zane asked.

"Of course," Bonnie said as Duster chuckled. "We were just waiting for Dr. Russell to get here to have you both work as a team for a time."

"But we need you to do something first," Duster said, "assuming Dr. Russell agrees to our offer of setting up the data bank."

"What's that?" Zane asked.

"We need you to take Dr. Russell with you back to Step Two. To establish her there."

Belle watched as Zane opened his mouth, then closed it, then opened it again, but nothing came out.

"We would like you both to work from here in Step One level. But it would be better for both of you to be safe from any kind of accident."

Zane just sat back, clearly shocked at something Belle flat didn't understand.

"Mind explaining what you mean by Step One and Step Two to me?" Belle asked.

"The institute, through time," Bonnie said, "was designed by all of us with the idea that it would continue to grow. "We are sitting in Step One time. Think of it as a staging area for anything back to 1880 when the institute was constructed."

Belle nodded, so Bonnie went on.

"Step Two is exactly one hundred years in the future, staying always exactly 100 years in the future from this first step time."

Belle sort of just stared at her.

Bonnie smiled and went on. "A traveler from Step Two can only travel back to this step and no farther back. From Step Two, the traveler must move to a Step One area of the institute and jump from there, as Zane did today with you."

She glanced at Zane, shocked. "You are from a hundred years in the future?"

He nodded. "I was supposed to be here working undercover."

Belle had no idea what to think of that, so she turned back to Bonnie. "How many step platforms are there into the future?"

"At the moment there are four," Bonnie said.

Zane sat forward on that one, clearly surprised. "The institute actually goes two hundred years beyond Step Two? I had heard that but never had it confirmed."

"It does," Duster said.

Dawn looked at Belle. "If Zane died right now, right here, he would return to his time very much alive. And all the time he has spent back here, all the years of setting up a background cover and writing books and so on would have only cost him two minutes and fifteen seconds in his real timeline."

"That's why we want Zane to take you to his timeline," Dawn said, "and then the both of you return instantly to this timeline just after you left here. We want you to be based in the future as well, so if something happens to you here, you will be fine."

Belle opened her mouth, but not a thought or a word happened.

She had not often experienced a complete blank, but at the moment, that was how she was thinking.

"I didn't know a person could travel forward in time," Zane said.

"With help from a person from the future, they can," Bonnie said. "Just as you can take clothes and notebooks and money back with you, by simply holding another person's hand, you can take them with you as well."

Zane just nodded. "And that establishes the person in the future timeline?"

"It does," Duster said. "The person becomes a part of that timeline."

"So that's why entire lines of DNA start and suddenly stop," Belle said, finally starting to get a grasp on her mind again.

"Yes," Dawn said. "it is why, as your great, great grandparents, you could not find our record before that time. We did not exist in this timeline before then."

"So how many are traveling in time?" Belle asked.

"At any given moment maybe a hundred," Duster said.

Belle laughed. "Then you have a problem. I have already found, in just

getting started with my research, over ten thousand different dead-end genetics lines."

Now it was time for Bonnie and Duster to be shocked.

"So I need to get one thing clear in my mind, if that's possible at the moment," Belle said, doing her best to form a simple thought.

"Go ahead and we'll try to answer anything," Dawn said, glancing with a worried expression at Bonnie and Duster.

"Say I was a traveler from Step Four," Belle said, "and I went to Step Three and then jumped again with a new crystal to Step Two and then jumped again through a new crystal to here and then jumped again through yet another crystal into the past."

Bonnie nodded.

Belle went on. "So I could live a thousand lifetimes in the past from here, with only two minutes and fifteen seconds passing in each lifetime. Correct?"

All three of the founders of the institute facing her nodded.

"And then I could live thousands of full lifetimes in this stage and only two minutes and fifteen seconds will have passed in Stage Two, when I returned, for each lifetime back here. And so on. Correct?"

"Correct," Dawn said. "But you don't need to be from Stage Four, just Stage Two will do it, since you could live a thousand lifetimes from one life here, then jump to Stage Two and reset for another two minutes and live another thousand lifetimes. And so on and so on. Timelines are infinite."

Belle glanced at the now haunted look in Zane's eyes.

Then she looked at the three founders of this incredible place. They all sat gazing at her.

"In other words," Belle said, "to work on a life's dream project, you are offering me all the money I will ever need, all the technology, and basic immortality."

All three nodded.

Belle laughed, shaking her head. "You drive a hard bargain, but I think I'll take the job."

All three of the founders and Zane clapped and Zane leaned over and kissed her on the cheek.

CHAPTER SIXTEEN

June 9th, 2020
Boise, Idaho

ZANE HAD NEVER been so shocked in all his life to learn that the founders knew he had been in Step One time for all these years. He supposed it shouldn't have surprised him, since he had had to come back through the Step Two room, and then go out a secret tunnel into the eastern mansion and then out. Clearly they had security on that room, as they should.

He still sat with the three founders and Belle in the huge cavern called The Living Room. He had almost finished his hot chocolate and the chill was gone that he had felt from the trip back to 1885.

And Belle had accepted the job they had offered her.

Now they had mentioned they wanted him for an exploration into a cavern. He now had managed to get his shocked mind back thinking and he had a few questions because he had a hunch which cavern they were talking about. And no one but the founders even knew where it was located.

"If I may," Zane asked, "Are you four all established in future stages as well?"

"All founders of the institute have been established in Stage Four," Duster said. "But we are all working and living here in Stage One."

"I can't imagine we will ever work or live in any other stage," Bonnie said. "I love jumping back to the past from here far too much."

The other two nodded to that.

"And there are fourteen founders?" Zane asked.

"There are," Dawn said. "Seven couples. You will eventually meet all of them."

Duster leaned forward, a very serious look on his face. "I have another surprise for both of you."

"Damn, not sure how much more my poor brain can handle in surprises," Belle said.

Zane laughed and glanced at Belle. "I'm game if you are."

She smiled. "Sure, just been offered the dream job, unlimited money, and immortality. What's one more thing on the pile?"

Everyone laughed, then Duster said, "We want you both to join the founders."

Zane rocked back and sat staring at Duster.

"Not at all sure what that means," Belle said.

"With you doing the genetics project," Dawn said to Belle, "and Zane doing what we hope he will help us with, we are going to need to take you both to the crystal cavern."

"When I left Step Two, there were only fourteen founders," Zane said.

"And when you return," Dawn said, "common knowledge will be that there are sixteen."

"You'll understand how that all works later," Duster said. "No point in getting sidetracked on this."

"So what does being a founder mean?" Belle asked.

"It means that eventually we will establish you in Stage Four so nothing that happens here or even hundreds of years in the future can kill you," Duster said.

"And it means that you will be one of only sixteen people who know where the crystal cavern is at," Dawn said.

"And it means that you will sit in with the founders meetings as we all try to set the course of this institute into the future."

"Holy shit," Zane said, stunned beyond words. This was only his second trip back into the past from Step Two.

He felt young, a baby.

Zane sat forward, staring at Duster. Then he pointed to Belle. "One short trip from here into the past."

Then Zane pointed to his own chest. "Only two trips back from Step Two and the short trip back earlier into the past. So why the two of us? We are babies compared to all of you."

Duster pointed off at the crystal door. "In two hours in there, at two minutes and fifteen seconds a trip, and living about thirty years in the past per trip, you could live over a thousand years. That's in two hours."

Zane nodded and Belle sort of gasped. He had been wrapping his mind around the realities of this kind of travel now for years here, knowing that in Stage Two, he would only be gone a few minutes.

"We don't need you to have vast amounts of years," Duster said, his dark eyes boring through Zane. "You can get that quickly if you want. We need your fresh look at things, your ability in understanding deep caves, and Belle's ability to understand the complexities of genealogy and genetics."

Zane nodded. "Thank you."

"Yes," Belle said. "Thank you."

Silence filled the large living room cavern for a few moments, then Duster smiled. "You two ready to get to work?"

Zane glanced at Belle, who was smiling.

"I am so ready," Belle said. "I want to get going before I wake up from this dream and realize I am still on the plane headed here."

Zane stood and extended his hand to help her up. "Whatever you do, for my sake, please don't wake up."

She took his hand and he helped her off the couch as the others stood as well, all laughing.

And the feeling of her hand in his felt wonderful. It took him an extra second to let go.

And Belle didn't seem to mind at all.

CHAPTER SEVENTEEN

June 9th, 2020
Boise, Idaho

"LET'S GET YOU established in Stage Two first," Duster said to Belle.

He turned and headed in a different direction from the living room than where they had come in or gone to the other crystals that had taken her into the past.

Belle still felt shocked. In fact, she was beyond shocked and all this just seemed so impossible. If she hadn't seen Warm Springs Avenue for herself in 1885, in a snowstorm, she never would be believing any of this.

And even now this seemed hard to grasp. But she wasn't fighting it anymore now, but going along and trying to learn. And she had a hunch that the learning was going to take more years than she could now imagine.

"The institute is divided up into four very secure sections," Dawn said as they walked across the big living room cavern. "You saw the Step One sections of supplies and crystal rooms when we jumped back to 1885 earlier."

Belle nodded. She knew those were in the other direction from where they were headed.

"The crystals in Step One were put into place from the cavern in 1880," Dawn said. "Step Two crystals were brought from the cavern three years ago."

"So no one from Step Two can travel back to the past, but only this far," Zane said. "But how do you block the crystals from taking them back into the cavern?"

Duster laughed. "Bonnie and I designed the devices inside those boxes. Trust me when I say they can't be tampered with or changed and they limit the length of time anyone can go back in any fashion. For example, if we allowed someone from this stage to go back before 1880, they would end up in an underground cavern with no way to get out that we know of."

Belle nodded. That made sense. Containing all travel to 100 years segments, like changing planes on a long flight.

"Before Step Two was founded," Dawn said, "all Step One crystals in the Step One rooms were returned to the cavern."

"Let me show you Step Three transport rooms," Duster said, reaching a large metal door and unlocking it.

"That needs to be better protected," Zane said, pointing to the big metal door and how easy it would be for someone to get through it.

Duster smiled. "Not really. There's nothing in here."

Belle watched as Duster opened the big metal door and walked into a huge cavern carved from the stone. A few lights came up as they entered, but it was clear the cavern was completely empty.

"This is the staging area for the level three travelers coming into Step Two time," Duster said. "The rooms of crystals and such will be beyond this, but they are all empty as well. They won't have crystals until Step Two time frame. It was also filled three years ago, but a hundred years into the future."

"And so on," Dawn said. "Let's get to Step Two and let Belle get established so she is safe in this time."

They all left the empty cavern and Duster locked the door.

"Finding it hard to imagine that being safe part," Belle said as they headed toward yet another side of the large living cavern.

"You'll come to accept it more and more as time goes on and with more trips into the past," Dawn said.

They reached another metal door and Zane knew exactly what was beyond this door. A lot of clothing for this time period, money, information devices, and so on. He was stunned the first time he saw it a hundred years in the future and was again stunned when Duster opened the door and the lights came up bright.

It looked like a giant department store had been set up in a vast cavern. Everything a person living in this time might need was provided.

"Wow," Belle said. "Does Walmart know you bought one of their entire stores?"

"More inventory than one of their stores," Duster said, his voice just matter of fact as he headed through the supply area and toward the crystal room doors on the other side.

Zane knew he had come into this timeline in the fifth room down, using a crystal tucked clear to the back.

Duster walked directly to the door and opened it. The lights came up on the narrow room with wire down both sides protecting anyone from touching any of the crystals in carved niches in the stone.

"How did you know I was here?" Zane asked as all four of them headed down the long row of tables and machines toward the only machine in the back hooked to a crystal.

"I had your director send you," Duster said without looking around.

"Oh," Zane said. He didn't know what else to say.

"So why did you have him stay hidden for all the years?" Belle asked, glancing at Zane and then back at Duster as they reached the machine attached to a crystal in one wall.

"It was a sort of test," Duster said. "And we needed him to get used to this time period and establish himself here as well."

Duster looked at Zane with those intense eyes. "Did it work?"

"Not sure about the test part," Zane said, "but I like this time period. And I feel fairly established."

Duster shrugged. "So it worked. And that's why we made you this offer."

Zane nodded. Then glanced at the wooden box and then at Belle before turning back to Duster. "May I show Belle Warm Springs Avenue in my time?"

"Sure," Duster said. "But not much more. We need you both back here and no point in taking too many chances."

Zane nodded and turned to Belle, who was looking both worried and excited.

"Ready to take another trip?" Zane asked.

"I think so," she said. Her eyes looked worried again.

Zane quickly picked up a thick glove on the desk. "What time is it exactly?" he asked as he put on the glove.

"Three-forty in the afternoon on June 9th, 2020," Dawn said and Duster checked a pocket watch and nodded.

"We'll be back in ten minutes," Zane said.

"We'll be in the living room waiting," Duster said.

Zane reached out his hand to Belle.

"Be close together," Duster said as Belle took Zane's hand.

Zane loved the feeling of touching her skin and as Duster said that, he pulled her close.

"Put your other arm around my neck," Zane said. "And hang on. I've never done this before."

"You are not encouraging me," Belle said as she hugged him with her other arm and he pulled one wire from the box.

And Duster and Bonnie and Dawn and Madison disappeared.

After nine years, he was back in his own time, just over two minutes since he had left.

His own time was the last place he really wanted to be.

But at least Belle was hugging him and that felt wonderful.

CHAPTER EIGHTEEN

June 9th, 2120
Boise, Idaho

BELLE FELT STUNNED that the four founders had just vanished. That meant that she and Zane really had traveled exactly one hundred years into the future.

How was that even possible?

She was still holding his hand and hugging his neck.

He dropped the wire and turned slightly to her. They were very close and she loved being this close.

"That wasn't so bad, was it?" he asked, smiling at her.

She slowly eased her grasp around his shoulders and neck and then let go of his hand, something she really didn't want to do.

He took off the glove, then offered his hand again. "Come on, let me show you just a little of my original time, and now your time as well. Then we can jump back to the founders."

His hand made her feel less afraid. "I would like that."

Hand-in-hand, they headed back along the wooden tables and the fenced-in walls of crystals.

On the other side of the door was the same massive room that looked like the entire contents of a few major stores.

They headed through that and out into the big living room cavern. She could hear talking coming from the living room area, and some laughing, and someone was cooking what smelled like pepperoni pizza that made her stomach growl.

"Wow, that smells good," Zane said as they headed, hand-in-hand to the right along the edge of the big living room and to an elevator.

She loved that he was holding her hand and guiding her. It made her feel about a thousand times more secure than she would have felt alone or with one of the founders.

Zane got on board the elevator and said simply "Street Level."

The metal doors slid closed and then an instant later, without feeling of movement at all, the doors opened again and Zane pulled her toward the wall door.

"That was nifty," she said as they stepped off into a closed room.

"Some things just speed up with time is all," Zane said, laughing.

Zane quickly checked through a security device and then smiled at her. "All clear."

They stepped through the door and right into the same front lobby where they had met.

Belle was stunned once again. It was the same old desk, same period furniture, same fireplace.

"Creepy, isn't it?" Zane said. "We've traveled over two hundred years in time and this room still looks the same no matter where we are."

"How is that possible?" Belle asked.

"Founders make sure it is maintained I guess," Zane said.

He led her toward the large wooden front door and then outside into a warm summer afternoon.

The porch looked the same, with the same period furniture on it. The front lawn looked the same as well with the wall and hedge covering it. But through the old trees she could see a modern building just up the road. That building seemed to be all tinted brown glass and looked almost invisible against the trees and bushes around it.

Zane still had ahold of her hand and gently urged her to come with him down the walk and toward the street. The air smelled fresh and had a faint hint of cut grass to it.

"Just over two hundred and thirty-five years ago we froze our asses off on this sidewalk," he said.

She remembered well. This was the third time she had been on this sidewalk. The first time in 2020, the second time in 1885, and now, supposedly in 2120.

She was going to need a lot of time to get used to all this and even absorb this happening.

Zane got to the gate, stated his name, and the gate opened automatically, and hand-in-hand they stepped through.

On the other side of the gate he let go of her hand, letting her just turn as she wanted to stare at the sight in front of her.

The wide and very busy five-lane street from a hundred years before was almost completely gone. Belle felt as if she was walking into a park with some gently curving paths winding through younger trees and shrubs.

On the paths were wide cars not much different in design from sleek cars of a hundred years before. They were all varying colors and makes. Only the cars passing them were clearly a lot larger and made no noise at all.

None.

They all moved at a constant rate and kept an exact distance apart.

"Electric cars that don't need to be driven," Zane said. "Some are large enough to get up and walk around in as you are traveling."

Then he pointed upward to what looked like an elevated cable. As she watched, a bullet-shaped transport longer than an old bus flashed past, also silently.

Then a moment later another one going the other direction on a cable flashed by, again silently.

"Mass transit covers most all areas of this city," he said.

Then he pointed to the west along Warm Springs Avenue. Through the trees she could see towering skyscrapers that now dominated the Boise downtown area.

"Boise restricted sprawl growth about eighty years ago and went upwards more than out," Zane said. "It's an amazing place."

"Looks like it," Belle said, slowly staring around at the silently moving cars and the park-like setting that used to be a busy street. Some old, some newer buildings lined the far side of the park. Everything she would see was perfectly maintained.

Through the park-like area, numbers of people walked, enjoying the warm day. And clearly the fashions of one hundred years in the future were not much different, since most everyone she saw seemed to be either dressed in business casual or jeans and light shirts.

She and Zane did not look out of place in the slightest.

"So most roads have become parks?" Belle asked, glancing at Zane.

"All city streets," Zane said. "When the self-driving electric cars took over, the cities started tearing up the old roads, building the new narrow roads with the embedded tracks for the cars, and turning the rest of the area into parks."

Belle suddenly realized what was missing. "There's no place to park?"

"Cars are all stored underground in big facilities in every neighborhood," Zane said. "Most of them under these streets. You need your car, you just push a button and it will appear in front of your home in less than a minute."

"Wow," Belle said. She was flat stunned.

And impressed.

And she basically lived in this time now. She was going to have to learn a lot to even get by here.

"Sure looks like everything developed nicely in the last hundred years," Belle said, once again scanning the beautiful neighborhood.

Zane shrugged. "Looks wonderful standing here on Warm Springs Avenue in a fairly protected town of Boise, Idaho. But there were numbers of wars over the last hundred years, more than I want to think about, actually."

Belle didn't like the sound of that at all, but didn't ask any more.

Zane went on. "Plus a huge earthquake wiped out a large part of the west coast about forty years ago, but that has rebuilt. And a couple of major cities were hit with bombs, but have rebuilt now as well. A couple major plagues wiped out millions through Asia and Africa before being stopped. World's population is now lower than it was a hundred years ago. So not a smooth road to all this."

Belle nodded, not even beginning to absorb some of the tragedy he had just outlined. "I have a lot to learn about my new time."

"I'll be glad to help," Zane said, turning and smiling at her.

She offered her hand. "I'll take you up on that. But I think for the moment we need to get back to Step One time."

He took her hand and smiled.

Damn she was enjoying that smile and the feeling of his hand in hers.

She was standing a hundred years in the future and had only known Zane for less than twelve hours. None of this was possible, yet she seemed to be experiencing it.

They turned and hand-in-hand went back through the gate and up the sidewalk toward the institute.

She knew this all had to be a dream. She just knew it, but it was her dream and until she woke up, she was going to keep on holding Zane's hand.

PART THREE
The Cavern

CHAPTER NINETEEN

June 16th, 2020
Boise, Idaho

THE LAST WEEK had gone so fast, Zane could hardly remember most of it. He and Belle had gotten back from 2120 and spent the evening talking with Bonnie and Duster and Dawn until his brain was fried.

Then he and Belle had walked to a nearby store to get her some food for her kitchen, then he had helped her get the bags of food into her kitchen and then had left her to settle into her new place.

She had looked as tired and shocked as he felt about everything that happened. And he was used to time travel, so he could only imagine how she was really feeling.

And the next morning when he rang her doorbell, he was very happy that she was still here.

The next six days had been mostly the two of them with Dawn and Bonnie, learning as much as they could handle about the institute, the history of the institute, and so on.

Zane had hoped that he and Belle would have more time just together, but except for walking to and from the institute, they hadn't had much alone time at all. Zane hoped that was going to change at some point.

With every day, he had grown more and more attracted to Belle. And she seemed to be feeling the same way toward him, since she often just took his hand for comfort.

Finally, now, at three in the afternoon of the seventh day since Belle had come through the front door of the institute, they were back in the big living room area cavern, sipping on Diet Cokes and munching on a fruit plate that Dawn had made. They were sitting in the couch and chair grouping that was closest to the kitchen area. The stone fireplace had no fire in it and no one else was around.

Zane knew the coming conversation was going to be important because Dawn and Bonnie were now joined by Duster and Madison. Director Parks had joined the group as well.

"It's time to talk about the next step," Duster said, leaning forward slightly, staring at first Zane, then Belle with his dark eyes. He was wearing a gray silk shirt and jeans and cowboy boots. There was no sign of his long coat or cowboy hat.

Zane only nodded.

"Not sure I'm ready for much, but willing to learn," Belle said.

"First, Dr. Russell," Duster said to Belle, "When you did the research into genealogy that you have already started, you said you found more dead-ends such as Dawn and Madison here as your grandparents?"

Zane had no idea what she was being asked, and she seemed confused as well.

"Let me put this a different way," Bonnie said. "You could find no evidence at all of any existence of Dawn and Madison as your grandparents before they appeared at the lodge. Is that correct?"

Belle nodded. "Yes."

"So have you, in your preliminary research, found many others like that?"

"Oh, sure," Belle said. "More than ten thousand, but I always assumed, as I did with you two, that it was just my inability to track back into the rough records of that time in history."

Zane had no idea where this line of questioning was going, but his stomach felt twisted, which means the founders had a hunch about something, and they were after some sort of confirmation.

Bonnie nodded to Belle's answer, but Duster sat forward even more. "Would you even have a rough percentage of genealogy lines that ended in that sort of dead-end? Or better put, a sudden start."

"It wouldn't be accurate," she said, "but give me a few years with the equipment and resources you have talked about and I'll be able to give you that number. Plus I am sure it will depend on the time period involved. Finding records in 1900 is much more difficult than finding records in 1950."

"Have you run across such sudden starts of lines in 1950s and forward?" Duster asked.

Belle glanced at Zane. She looked as puzzled as he felt.

"Sure," she said, turning back to face Duster. "From 1950 forward about five percent of all lines I have tried to trace had such sudden starts. But again, more than likely, I did not have the right equipment or the right records."

With that Duster sat back.

Zane could tell he did not look happy.

"Why?" Belle asked.

"Because I've been afraid," Duster said, "that our mine entrance is not the only entrance into the crystal caverns. And we are not the only group traveling in time."

"Oh," Belle said, sitting back against the couch.

Suddenly Zane understood exactly why he was sitting here.

"So we're going looking for more openings?" Zane said. "From the inside of the big caverns."

"We are," Duster said, nodding.

"And what are we going to do if we find them?" Zane asked.

"Block them before anyone can start using them," Parks said, his voice intense.

"Not sure if that will be possible," Duster said.

Parks just shrugged. They clearly had had that discussion already.

"So that means we're going back to 1880," Zane said.

"From here we'll jump to 1900," Duster said. "We'll get supplies and pack horses and such and get them into the cavern. Then we'll jump back another twenty years from there."

"Sort of a small step," Zane said, liking that idea. "So we don't always reset to here."

"Exactly," Bonnie said.

"How big are these caverns?" Belle asked.

"We don't know exactly," Bonnie said.

"I believe they circle the globe along the 42nd parallel," Duster said.

"We don't know for sure," Bonnie said, looking at her husband.

"But that's what the math says," Duster said.

Zane had one problem. "I can't imagine a complex of caves stretching that long would not have been discovered in my time, or two hundred years into the future, for that matter which you would have known about as well."

Both Bonnie and Duster nodded.

Then Duster said, "The complex of crystal caverns we believe exists in a dimension just off of any normal dimension. We tried to plot them with ground penetrating equipment at one point and couldn't even see our main cavern."

"But entrances are the links," Bonnie said. "When Duster's distant relatives broke through into the big crystal cavern, he basically anchored that part of the cavern system to our timelines."

"The math backs it all up," Duster said.

Zane sat back, trying to wrap his mind around what he had just heard. So he was going to explore a complex of massive caverns in the past, caverns that actually didn't exist in any real time. That was damn hard to believe or imagine.

But he also couldn't imagine sitting in a big cavern one hundred years in the past either, talking with people who looked his age, but who had lived many, many thousands of years.

So he figured anything was possible.

CHAPTER TWENTY

June 16th, 2020
Boise, Idaho

AFTER TALKING WITH the founders for a few more hours about the coming project, Zane and Belle walked downtown along Warm Springs Avenue in the warm evening air, shaded under the large trees that lined both sides of the street. The walk was just about as comfortable as any walk Belle could remember taking.

She and Zane just seemed to fit together, and the more time she spent with him, the more she really liked him and admired his quick mind and fearless nature when it came to things that just scared her to death.

They were walking hand-in-hand, as they tended to do the last few days, and she loved the feel of his skin against hers. The slight breeze smelled of hot sagebrush and as they neared the Brooks Garden Restaurant the smell was joined by garlic and fresh bread.

They had eaten here three times over the last week together, and they both loved it. The young hostess wearing a dark blouse and black pants behind the counter recognized them and showed them to a private table near the back, surrounded by plants and high-backed booths.

Belle hadn't realized just how hungry she was until they walked in and sat down. Before the hostess could leave, Belle asked her for a basket of the fresh bread.

"I was thinking the same thing," Zane said, smiling.

The bread seemed to just appear on their table a moment later and as Belle was smothering a piece with honey butter, she asked Zane, "So what is it going to be like exploring a cave complex that large?"

"Honestly," Zane said, working on his own piece of bread, "more than likely impossible. But I won't know until I've seen it."

She nodded. "Sounds like the problem is going to be food."

"Among thousands of other problems," Zane said. "Tomorrow, I plan on having Bonnie and Dawn describe the main cavern as closely as possible. Then I'm going to have Director Parks do the same thing. After that, I'll be able to at least start to form a plan and get ready as much as I can."

"I'd like to sit in on those discussions," Belle said and then took a bite of her bread, letting the wonderful soft taste of butter and freshly baked bread melt in her mouth.

Before Zane could even answer, the waiter showed up and they both ordered their favorite salads. She went with the Cobb salad and he ordered the chef's salad. And they both ordered iced teas as well.

After the waiter left, she turned to face Zane across the table. "And not only do I want to listen in on the description of the cave, I want to go with you."

He frowned. "I would love that, but don't you have a massive project to start?"

"We'll only be gone for a few minutes, remember?" she said, laughing.

He almost blushed, then smiled. "Forgot, and if we start from the institute, we can go back a hundred times into the caverns and yet still only be gone from here for a few minutes one day."

"Exactly," she said. "And besides wanting to spend all that time with you, I can really get to understand what I am facing on my genealogy project."

"I would love to have you along," Zane said, smiling. "It might be dangerous, but again, I suppose that won't matter."

"I am willing to take that risk of some pain," she said. "And I love caves."

He nodded. "I would love to have you along."

"Thank you," she said. Now that was decided. Now she had one more thing to get out of the way.

"You know," she said, smiling at him. "You have never invited me to see your apartment."

He sort of opened his mouth, then closed it, shaking his head and smiling. "I would be glad to show you my apartment at any point."

"How about right after dinner?" she asked, enjoying the stunned look on his handsome face.

"Any specific area of the apartment you really want to see?" he asked, trying not to smile.

"I was thinking that since you spend most of your time there in the bedroom, that would be the most interesting place."

He laughed that wonderful, deep laugh she had come to love over the last week.

"I also spend time in the shower," he said.

"We can start there," she said.

"Right after dinner?" he asked.

"Right after dinner," she said.

"How fast can you eat?"

"Damned fast," she said, laughing with him and enjoying the smile on his face. "But don't ask for the check just yet. I'm hungry."

CHAPTER TWENTY-ONE

June 17th, 2020
Boise, Idaho

ZANE AWOKE SLOWLY to the morning sun streaming in his bedroom window. Belle lay stretched out naked beside him, one hand touching his chest, her other arm covering her eyes from the light.

The sheet was only pulled up to just above her waist and her dark nipples were slightly hard. Her skin was fantastically smooth and soft and seemed flawless.

Last night they had barely made it to the shower before they made love for the first time. It had been intense and fast and hard, and he could never remember ever feeling like that with any woman, ever.

Then they had finished their shower, making sure the soap got a great workout as they explored each other's bodies. That was going to be an hour he would remember fondly, and vividly, for the rest of his life.

Then they had crawled onto his bed and made love for the next hour, going slow and easy and again ending with an intensity that he could have never imagined before.

They just fit together in all ways it seemed.

"Enjoying the view?" she asked without moving her arm away from covering her eyes.

"Very much," he said, easing the sheet down even more so that she was lying there basically naked.

Her body was stunning. Trim and in shape, with narrow hips and skin that felt almost like silk to him.

He stroked her stomach, moving his hand gently from her crotch to her breasts and then back again.

She moaned slightly after a moment, and then without warning, she swung over and on top of him, kissing him harder than she had done last night.

Fifteen passionate minutes later, they were once again headed back to the shower.

And forty minutes later they were dressed.

While she went to her apartment to get fresh clothes, he had managed to cook them both a small breakfast of eggs, toast, and summer fruit salad.

When she came back in she was laughing. "I love that almost no one is here in this complex. The walk to my apartment didn't even feel embarrassing."

"So you took a walk of shame in college, huh?" he asked, laughing.

"Only once," she said. "Hung over, wearing a dress completely out of place for where I was at, mad at myself for sleeping with such an idiot. How about you?"

"Only once as well," he said. "And as with yours, alcohol poisoning fogged my judgment."

"I hope nothing was foggy last night," she said, smiling as she sat down at the counter and he slid a plate of food toward her along with a glass of orange juice.

"Nothing foggy about that at all," he said, moving around the counter and kissing her hard again until she pushed him away.

"Hungry," she said. "And you keep that up, these wonderful-smelling eggs are going to get cold."

"A price eggs must pay at times," he said. But he moved around and served himself some eggs and fruit salad before sitting down across the counter from her. He was hungry as well.

After a moment he looked up at her. "Does this mean we only need to pack one tent on the excursion into the caverns?"

She laughed and he loved the sound of that. "So because you don't want us to carry two tents, you are asking me to move in with you after just one week of knowing me?"

"Yeah, pretty much," he said. "Damned tents can get heavy."

Again she laughed. "I guess I'll suffer for the expedition."

And he loved the sound of that as well.

CHAPTER TWENTY-TWO

June 25th, 2020
Boise, Idaho

FOR A WEEK, Zane and Duster worked on the plans for the expedition into the caverns and how they would do it over the next week while Belle worked with Dawn and Bonnie to try to track down as many of the family starts as they could trace with the information they had to try to find a pattern.

Belle had figured that since the pattern of the sudden starts of genealogy birth-lines around this entrance to the caverns was in the West, mostly focused in the Pacific Northwest, that other sudden genealogy starts might also be clear given some data.

She stayed focused on areas along the 42nd parallel as Bonnie and Duster suggested, and found one clear start-up cluster of genealogy lines in North and South Dakota.

When they told Duster and Zane, all Duster said was, "That's a hell of a hike underground."

Belle had to agree with that.

"One other thing," she said. "If an opening there is similar to the mine here, you may not find it in 1880. The lines don't really start until the 1940s."

They talked for a few more minutes in the kitchen area when Belle finally decided to ask the question that had been bothering her about all this.

"Why is it so bad that others know of time travel and the crystal caverns?"

Duster glanced at Bonnie who nodded.

"Time is very much like a river," Duster said. "In the overall sense of things, it is almost impossible to divert beyond a few alternate timelines. But it is possible, given enough time and focus."

"Are you saying something has happened in the future?" Belle asked, suddenly scared more than she wanted to admit.

"Besides all the normal events through history," Duster said, "2120 is fine, as you saw and Zane grew up in."

Zane was looking very worried, but he was too far away down the counter for Belle to take his hand.

"So what happened?" Zane asked.

"We screwed up," Bonnie said.

Duster nodded. "We published our findings on time travel in every journal and magazine that would take our articles about the nature of time and energy and matter being connected."

"We are quickly going back and pulling those research papers from timelines," Bonnie said. "We were foolish."

"But we will never get them all," Duster said. "And by 2320, a dictator using time travel through cavern crystals is controlling the world. It is not a pretty place to live."

"Boise was leveled in an attack looking for the institute," Bonnie said. "Millions died. In 2320, we never emerge from the caverns here. And there are only a few hundred of us left, doing our best to travel back in time to figure out how to reverse what happened."

"So that's why the importance of the genealogy project," Belle said. "To find and track those starting points."

Duster nodded. "Just as you gave us a lead to the Dakotas. Those crystals need to stay protected. And the theory of time travel needs to remain controlled and only a theory to the general population."

Belle looked at the worried look on Zane's face.

And there was not a thing she could say.

CHAPTER TWENTY-THREE

July 10th, 2020
Boise, Idaho

TWO WEEKS LATER they were all finally ready to go. Zane stood beside the table in the Step One crystal room as Duster hooked up the wires to a crystal that had never been used before. Belle stood beside him, holding his hand.

Duster was in his long coat and cowboy hat and boots. Bonnie and Belle and Zane would dress in time-appropriate clothing in the big supply room when they got to the other side.

Zane was both excited and scared to death. The caverns and being underground didn't worry him much, but being in 1900 sure did.

And that's where they were headed first, to July 10th, 1900. One hundred and twenty years in the past.

Bonnie and Duster would be with them headed to the old mine. But then Bonnie and Duster would wait in 1900 in the crystal cavern as Zane and Belle jumped back ten years in the crystal cavern to explore deep into the caverns on a first trip.

Duster had wanted to go along on the expedition, but all the founders had forbidden it. He and Bonnie were just too important to saving the world four hundred years in the future to risk.

And when Zane had asked in one dinner meeting what the risk was, since they couldn't die in the past, both Bonnie and Duster had looked worried and then said, "There are aspects about the crystal caverns we don't yet understand because we believe they exist in other dimensions of a sort."

"So we don't know about this not dying stuff inside the caverns is what you are saying?" Zane had asked, glancing at Belle.

Belle looked worried as well at that moment.

"We can't take the chance," Madison said, "of losing the math brains."

Zane understood that completely and had said, "Don't worry. Belle and I will figure out what can and can't be done in there."

And that had ended that conversation.

"Let's go," Duster said, closing the wire gate on the crystals and then setting the timer on the box.

Then he connected the two wires to the box wearing thick leather gloves.

Bonnie and Belle both moved up close to the box. Both were carrying large packs over the shoulders full of modern caving gear. Usually nothing modern was allowed back into the past, but Bonnie and Duster had made an exception for this trip.

Zane made sure his heavy pack was on his back and another pack was in his left hand and joined them.

Duster took off the gloves, shouldered a pack and picked up a large bag, then said, "On the count of three."

On three, Zane touched the wooden box at the same moment Belle did.

Nothing at all seemed to happen, which was normal.

They all stepped back and headed into the big supply room.

The year was 1900. And in a few days Zane was going to be headed into the cave of his life, from everything that had been described to him. And he felt the same excitement and nerves he felt before every big exploration.

CHAPTER TWENTY-FOUR

July 10th, 1900
Boise, Idaho

BEING A WOMAN of means in 1900 was no easy task to pull off, Belle finally decided, as she managed to not fall off her horse anywhere along the wagon trail that was Warm Springs Avenue going into Boise.

The clothes of this time alone were draconian in nature, and lucky Bonnie had said it was all right for Belle to keep on her modern underwear and a sports bra. Belle had packed a couple of the 1900 corsets, but had no intention of ever wearing one.

She had also never ridden a horse before. Ever. Growing up in suburban Phoenix had just not prepared her for riding horses, and she had never been one of the little girls who had wanted a pony. In fact, until this trip, she hadn't given horses even a single thought.

More than likely in 2020, she should have mentioned to someone she couldn't ride. But Bonnie and Duster and Zane had seemed to take her lack of knowledge and skill in stride, with only a few really bad jokes.

As Bonnie had said, "You'll be fine after a few days."

Bonnie was leading two pack-horses covered in supplies, so was Duster, and so was Zane. She was the only one riding alone in clothes far too tight and too heavy for the weather.

Ten minutes after climbing on her horse, the idea of a few days of riding seemed like an eternity she didn't want to live.

Belle's main annoyance at not being able to ride, besides the constant terror of falling off, was that she had to stay focused on the horse and not spend time looking around at the historical buildings and such they were passing.

So what she had noticed was that the day was going to be warm, that the trails were full of ruts and dusty, and that most places smelled like horse shit. And her horse seemed to have no problem in just plowing right through piles of other horse's shit, which kept the smell around her for the entire first hour of their ride.

She had barely made it through the streets of old Boise and out on the trail going west along the Boise River without falling off. And her legs were already starting to hurt.

Zane, on the other hand, looked as if he had been born on a horse. He rode high, looking handsome in his suit and vest and cowboy hat. He seemed to never pay much attention to the horse at all, but instead he looked at the sights, trying to get Belle to look up at times. Duster had said that he was impressed at Zane's horse skills at one point.

So was she. And very envious.

"A lot of entrances to caves needed to be packed into, even in 2120," Zane said in response to Duster. "Riding horses and leading pack horses is part of the caver skill set."

Belle had just shaken her head at that. There was so much about the man she was falling for that she didn't know. And from what Zane had said, they were going to have the time to get to know each other better in the long cave adventure.

And she was actually looking forward to that.

If she ever got off this damn horse and into the cave.

CHAPTER TWENTY-FIVE

July 11th, 1900
Above Silver City, Idaho

STANDING ON THE flat top of the mine tailings looking down at the mining town of Silver City was amazing. Zane couldn't believe he was actually here.

Beside him, holding his hand, Belle stared down the thousand feet at the old mining town as well. In 1900, Silver City was already on the decline, past its second boom cycle. But a good ten thousand people still lived in the valley below

them. The sounds of digging and chopping filled the air along with the distant sound of a piano playing from one of the saloons.

The trip from Boise had taken two days. The first day they had rode and then walked and then rode a little and then walked, finally camping near a hot springs on the banks of the Snake River.

At that point, after almost twelve hours of travel, Belle was in bad shape from the ride, the long walk, and the dry heat of the warm summer day. Bonnie and Duster looked right at home and not fazed in the slightest. Zane felt like he had gone through a tough workout, but he would be all right. It had been a while since he had spent that much time on a horse and he was feeling that in his legs.

Duster said he would take care of the horses while Bonnie started dinner and Zane helped Belle.

Zane had gotten some extra salt tablets in Belle and water and then had taken her down to the hot springs where he had enjoyed watching her get naked and moan as she crawled into the hot water.

He had joined her in the rock-lined hot-springs pool perched above the slowly moving Snake River below. It was a beautiful sight but Zane had a hunch Belle wasn't enjoying it that much. They had helped each other get clean and then get on fresh clothes and get back to camp.

Belle had managed to get some food and more water in her before crawling into their tent and passing out.

Zane must have looked worried, but Bonnie just laughed. "She'll be much better tomorrow."

And it turned out that she was.

Now, at three in the afternoon, after climbing almost a thousand feet up a hillside dotted with mine tailings, Zane and

Belle were at the old mine, standing on the mine's tailings, looking down at the old town below.

Behind them, a small wooden shack sat in front of a boarded-up mine entrance. Small rail tracks for ore cars ran from the mine out through the old shed and then to the front edge of the tailings.

From what Zane could tell, the area behind the boarded-up entrance had caved in, and he could see no way into the mine. He hoped that cave-in wasn't something new, but Bonnie and Duster hadn't seemed to notice it.

Zane had been in his share of old mines in his time. They were a thousand times more dangerous than any natural cave and he hadn't much liked them. Taking calculated risks in caves was one thing, going into old mines wasn't a calculated risk. It was just stupid.

Duster and Bonnie set up a fake camp quickly, with two tents and what looked like the remains of a firepit near the old shack.

All four of them had taken the packs and all the supplies from the pack horses, piling it near the entrance to the mine, then Duster had made sure the horses had enough feed and water for a day or so and had tied them off a short distance up the hill.

If anyone came by, it would look like a normal camp with the prospector out and away from the camp for the moment. It was a great cover, Zane had to admit.

Then Duster and Bonnie both took out binoculars and scanned the area in front of the mine and then the hillsides across the way. The hill slanted up steeply above the mine, but it turned to the right and ran out to another ridgeline across from the mine. The hills were all void of trees, leaving mostly only dried brush and other old mines.

From what Zane could see, none of the other mines in sight were active.

Out over the old town and a good two miles across the valley was another mountainside spotted with mines, but Zane doubted anyone could see them from that far.

"What are you looking for?" Belle had asked.

"Anyone looking this direction, or in sight of this mine," Duster had said.

After a moment Bonnie said, "Clear."

"You and Belle take as many packs and saddlebags as you can carry and get inside," Duster said, continuing to scan the mountains around them.

Belle suddenly looked worried and Zane only shrugged. They were not going through that old boarded up entrance, so he had no idea where inside was.

Bonnie indicated that Belle should get what she could carry from the pile as Duster kept scanning the hills around them.

Zane didn't exactly know what to do, so he helped Belle get a pack on her shoulder.

"Clear," Duster said after Bonnie told him they were ready.

Duster just kept scanning the hillsides above them for any movement at all.

Bonnie held up an old skeleton key and twisted the head on it, then tucked it away as a large rock beside them seemed to silently crack open and slide aside.

A big metal door on the inside of the rock opened and Bonnie started in.

Belle was surprised, but after a moment's hesitation, quickly followed, glancing back at Zane with a wide-eyed look.

The door closed silently and the big rock slid back into place.

"Wow," Zane said, shocked, as he just stared at where Belle had disappeared.

"Would have never guessed that was there."

"And no one has," Duster said. "In over four hundred years into the future."

CHAPTER TWENTY-SIX

July 11th, 1900
Above Silver City, Idaho

BELLE WAITED UNTIL the lights came up and then followed Bonnie into what looked to be an old mine tunnel. It had big wooden beams holding up the ceiling and ore car rails running down the middle. An old line of electrical lights were hanging along one wall, giving the place a gold tint which felt appropriate for a gold mine.

About thirty steps down the mine into the mountain, Belle could see where the tunnel curved to the right.

She didn't feel safe in here at all, but Bonnie seemed to think nothing of it, so she went in five paces, carrying all the bags and saddlebags and waited for Duster and Zane to join them.

After less than a minute, Zane came out of the metal door chamber behind the big rock, looking around. He was an expert at anything underground and Belle suddenly felt much better just seeing him and the fact that with a glance he broke out into a big smile.

Zane glanced back at Duster. "Great job reinforcing the old mine and making it look original."

"Thanks," Duster said. "Not many can spot that."

"I wouldn't want to be in here if you hadn't done it," Zane said, smiling at Belle.

And that smile made her feel much better.

Bonnie turned and headed into the mine. Belle was following, watching her step more than anything else for fear of tripping on the old mine ore car rails and dropping everything she was carrying.

Then, in front of her, Bonnie vanished.

"Now that's weird," Zane said from behind Belle.

"Wall there at the corner is a hologram," Duster said from behind Zane.

At that moment Bonnie came back about halfway through the wall and offered a hand to Belle, who took it.

"Close your eyes for a step and you'll be fine."

Belle did for three steps as Bonnie led her straight forward where it looked like the tunnel had turned.

Then Belle looked back at the surprised look and smile on Zane's face. Belle couldn't see the hologram from this side, but she knew where it was as Zane came forward and then closed his eyes for two steps right at a certain point.

Now the floor of the old mine was smooth since the rail car tracks had turned to the right.

"Nifty security feature," Zane said.

"Only one of many," Duster said. "I'll show them all to you a little later."

Belle loved the fact that Zane was smiling like a little kid in a candy store. Clearly being underground was his world and she actually wasn't feeling that uncomfortable either, which surprised her.

And having Zane smiling and enjoying himself made her feel better as well.

They went through another hologram that made the mine look like it dead-ended, and then into a big natural cavern about the same size as the living room cavern under the institute. Lights on the ceiling came on and lit the place with a bright white feel.

This was clearly their supply area, but nowhere near as large as the supply areas in the institute. Most of the wooden tables in here were empty. But there were still enough supplies to last for a very long time, of that Belle had no doubt.

There was one table along the right wall with a large gun rack over it, and racks and racks of men's suits and women's dresses from this period of time.

"Kitchen and bathroom areas back off to the left," Duster said, putting his saddlebags and packs onto one empty table.

Bonnie did the same, and Belle put what she was carrying on the table beside Bonnie's stuff. They would repack everything for the first excursion underground.

Zane put his stuff beside Belle's and then leaned over and kissed her.

"You two ready to see the crystal cavern before we go any farther?" Duster asked.

"Ready as I'll ever be," Belle said, smiling at Zane and winking.

Zane laughed and took her hand and the two of them turned to follow Duster toward another tunnel cut through the rock on the far side of the supply cavern.

At the end of that, Duster unlocked a big metal door and stepped through into what looked like bright pink light.

Belle and Zane followed and it took her about four steps into the huge cavern before she just stopped, unable to move.

"Holy shit!" Zane said softly beside her.

The cavern they had stepped into was so immense, she couldn't even begin to get a sense of how big it was. The floor was flat and brown dirt, but the walls towered far over their heads and every inch seemed to be covered with glowing pink quartz crystals.

Billions and billions of them of all sizes.

"Any of the largest football stadiums in the country in 2020 could fit inside of here and not touch the sides or ceiling," Duster said.

Belle just couldn't make her mind accept what she was seeing. It had a beauty to it that seemed to take all breath away.

She let go of Zane's hand and slowly turned around, trying to take it all in, but finding that impossible. The tiny door they had just come through seemed like nothing more than a dot on the massive wall of crystals that towered over her, arching upward to form the ceiling an impossible distance overhead.

Across the vast space she could see the cavern was attached to another massive cavern and then beyond that more and more until the massive caverns vanished into a pinpoint in the distance as if she were looking into a mirror reflected in another mirror.

She forced herself to take a deep breath and look down at the dirt floor and the footprints in the dirt to get her balance and bearing. Then she looked over to the right at a wooden table near one wall with a wooden box sitting on it and two wires lying on the ground.

"Mind if I sit down for a moment?" Belle asked, not waiting for an answer as she lowered herself to the floor of the cavern. She needed to feel some strength from the solidness of the floor. The vastness of the cavern was going to take some time for her mind to even pretend to grasp.

"Good idea," Zane said, sitting beside her.

Bonnie laughed. "Everyone sits down when they first see this place. Some, like you two, are just a little more dignified than others."

Belle was glad she was one of the dignified ones, but she had to admit, she didn't feel dignified in the slightest. She felt tiny and small and very, very much in awe of one of the great sights in the universe.

Stretching out in front of her and over her was the cavern where all energy and matter and time converged into a place of spectacular beauty and power.

Dignified in the face of all that just wasn't much of an option.

PART FOUR
Time Passes

CHAPTER TWENTY-SEVEN

July 11th, 1900
Above Silver City, Idaho

ZANE TOOK A deep breath and shouldered his backpack. Then he turned to make sure Belle was all right with her pack as well. She seemed to be fine.

Then he turned to Duster and Bonnie. Duster had on thick gloves and had connected the two wires to a crystal on the wall, then connected one end to the wooden box on the table. He had not connected the other wire just yet.

Over the last two hours, after first seeing the cavern, they had gone over the plan one more time while having a lunch in the modern kitchen area of the cavern.

All four of them were going to go back ten years to 1890, all carrying a vast amount of supplies and water to be left in the cavern near the table. They wanted to do that even with the supplies in the supply cavern just feet away, just in case. They were trying to cover all bases as much as they could.

Then Bonnie and Duster were going to stay in the packing area for one exact day, then Duster was to pull the wire from the machine.

Zane and Belle were going to set out walking into the caverns, trying to get in as far as they could in that same time before Duster pulled the wire.

In theory, pulling that wire would bring all four of them back to the wooden box in 1900.

In theory.

At one point in the planning process back in Boise, Zane had asked Duster, "You are afraid the time crystals won't work to pull us back because of dimensional distortions in the caverns, aren't you?"

Both Duster and Bonnie had nodded.

"So what do we do if that happens?" Zane had asked. "Where do we end up?"

Duster had looked at Bonnie and both of them had shrugged. "We honestly don't know. Our math can't account for all the dimensional distortions inside the cavern."

"More than likely you'll just stay in the same time you went back to, inside the same alternate timeline."

"In theory," Duster said. "But if that happens, we really don't know for sure."

"So why does the original table and device you have set up in the cavern work?" Belle had asked.

"We believe because it is near an entrance to this world," Bonnie had said.

"Grounded," Duster said.

So now that they were about to head out into the caverns, Zane had made sure that he and Belle had enough to eat to last them months if needed in the packs they were carrying. And most of the weight they were both carrying was water.

Also, all four of them had a bunch of extra supplies they were going to jump back with and then leave off to one side of the cavern. Duster and Zane had figured those extra supplies would be enough to almost get them to North Dakota if they came back and the mine tunnel entrance was gone for some reason.

If something happened to them inside these caverns, there was a very good chance that the living forever thing wouldn't apply. They had no safety net.

Now granted, Zane hadn't been used to living with that safety net of the immortality of time travel for very long. But he liked the idea and now thinking it might no longer apply in these caverns bothered him more than he wanted to admit.

Zane, in all his caving, had never gone into a cave that he wasn't sure would have an entrance after he got inside. He didn't actually mind that much, but the institute and the future needed Belle and risking her life suddenly just seemed foolish.

As they stood near the table, ready to go back the ten years in time, Zane turned to Duster and Bonnie, not letting himself look at Belle. "I'd like to change the plans some."

"A little late for that," Duster said, frowning.

"I want to try this alone first," Zane said. "Belle is needed by the institute for her work. I'm just a caver."

"No!" Belle said.

Zane had never heard such intensity in her voice before.

He turned to Belle and started to say something, but she held up her hand. The fire in her eyes was something.

"I understand what you are trying to do," she said. "But I have left clear instructions on what I know about genetics and my research and Bonnie and others can move it forward just fine. Our chances for survival go up when we are together, and besides, I seem to remember reading something in one of your books about this very topic. Didn't you say that a solo caver is a dead caver?"

Zane laughed and Duster chuckled.

"We stick with the plan," Belle said.

"Everyone get ready to touch the device on the count of three," Duster said, hooking up the last wire and then removing his glove.

Zane just looked at Belle and smiled. "You know I had to try."

"And I would have been disappointed if you hadn't," Belle said.

Again Duster chuckled and said, "One…"

CHAPTER TWENTY-EIGHT

July 11th, 1890
Deep Inside the Crystal Caverns

SHE AND ZANE had been walking at a steady pace for three hours now, deeper into the crystal caverns. The pace was comfortable for both of them and they had used one energy bar snack an hour ago and drank just enough water to keep them going without worry.

The temperature seemed to be a comfortable high sixties and the air was dry enough to help them stay cool but not sweat too much.

The floor so far had been slightly downhill and completely flat.

It had taken them almost twenty minutes to walk across the floor of the main cavern, through the massive arch between caverns that was higher than most bridges over rivers, and then into the second cavern.

At the archway, they had stopped and built up a small pile of dirt in the form of an arrow pointing back at the distant table and the tiny figures of Bonnie and Duster in the distance.

Now, after three hours, they were standing under yet another archway leading to another huge cavern. This had to be the tenth massive cavern at least that they had passed through. And not one inch of any wall that Belle had seen wasn't covered by the glowing pink crystals.

If the cavern hadn't been tested numbers of times by Duster and others for radiation, she would have been worried about what they were absorbing.

In the archway they stopped and Belle dug out the water they had been using while Zane pulled out a lighter and what looked like a stick. It didn't flame, but put off a white smoke.

Zane held the stick up and let the smoke rise in the air.

Belle knew that he was looking for some sort of breeze. Both Bonnie and Duster had said they had never felt a breeze in the crystal cavern, but Zane had insisted there had to be one, otherwise the atmosphere in the places would soon stale out. Something had to be moving the air.

The smoke moved in the direction they were headed gently and Zane nodded and snuffed out the stick.

"That a good sign I assume?" Belle asked, handing him the water bottle.

"A very good sign," he said, smiling at her. "Since these caverns we have been in are basically a dead-end run, I didn't expect much. But I've been feeling a little breeze, so that means we are getting close to the main run of caverns."

Belle nodded and put the bottle of water away in her pack after Zane took a small drink. In some of the planning sessions, after the caverns had been described to them, Zane had flat insisted that the cavern at the mine was the end cavern of a dead-end run.

And if the caverns were going to go all the way to the Dakotas along the forty-second parallel, then that made sense as well.

He and Zane made their little mound of dirt under the archway with the arrow pointing back in the direction they had come and moved on.

Three more caverns later they hit the main line of caverns.

And again, both of them had to sit down about four steps inside the big main cavern.

The cavern of crystals around them could hold every cavern they had walked through already and still have room for more. She figured it was large enough to hold all of Manhattan Island.

Easily.

The massive caverns they had been inside since the mine had only been a tiny side path.

And from where they were, just barely into this one cavern, she could see at least a hundred other side paths moving away like massive tunnels.

Nothing in Belle's imagination could have prepared her for this.

Nothing.

"Every decision, by every person in history," Zane said softly, as if talking in a normal voice in this sort of scene would be wrong. "And this is only a small part of them."

All Belle could do was sit there in the dirt, her mouth open, just staring.

CHAPTER TWENTY-NINE

July 11th, 1890
Deep Inside the Crystal Caverns

ZANE KNEW HE had met his match as a caver.

There was no sane way to move forward into the massive cave.

None, even though the floor was flat and the going would be easy, they would die in here.

It really was that simple.

Some of the crystals on the walls and hanging from the ceilings were larger than skyscrapers and had thousands and thousands of smaller crystals hanging off of them.

He took off his pack. "Dig us out something to eat if you wouldn't mind."

Belle nodded and turned from the incredible sight and took off her pack as well.

Zane needed to do some quick experiments to see if his hunch was right as to what was happening in front of them.

He pulled out his smoke stick and lit it. Smoke went straight up without being bothered in the slightest by a breeze.

"That what you expected?" Belle asked as he put the smoke stick away.

"In a cavern this size," he said, "that is the only thing that could happen. "Even a thousand openings wouldn't move the air in here. A single opening would be like turning on a fan in the Bronx and expecting someone to feel it in Manhattan."

She nodded as he took out his compass. As expected, it flat didn't work, so he tucked it away. His personal sense of direction, which had always been good even in the dark underground, told him the big cavern ran east to west.

And in the distance on both ends of the big cavern were massive other caverns he could barely see.

He then glanced at his watch. They had only been going now for just under five hours.

She handed him a beef sandwich that they had made for this first meal before leaving the supply cavern.

He took a bite and it tasted wonderful, the mustard just perfect on his. The taste helped calm him some, let his mind clear.

Belle turned around and sat beside him on the dirt floor, eating and staring in silence at the sight in front of them.

He tried to count the side entrances off the main chamber and lost track at around fifty. And those were the ones he could see. Some of them might stretch for a hundred miles before ending, some might only go one cavern deep.

But all of them could have openings out into the real world.

Or none of them might.

"This can't exist, can it?" Belle asked.

"Not in any real world of earth's crust that we know," Zane said. "As Bonnie and Duster had figured, all this must exist in some sort of space outside of real space."

Belle shook her head.

Zane just looked around. "This is all way beyond me, but I know for a fact no cavern like this one could exist in our planet's crust, let alone all the other ones we can see from here. This flat isn't a natural cavern in the slightest."

Now Available
from all your favorite booksellers in trade paper and electronic editions.

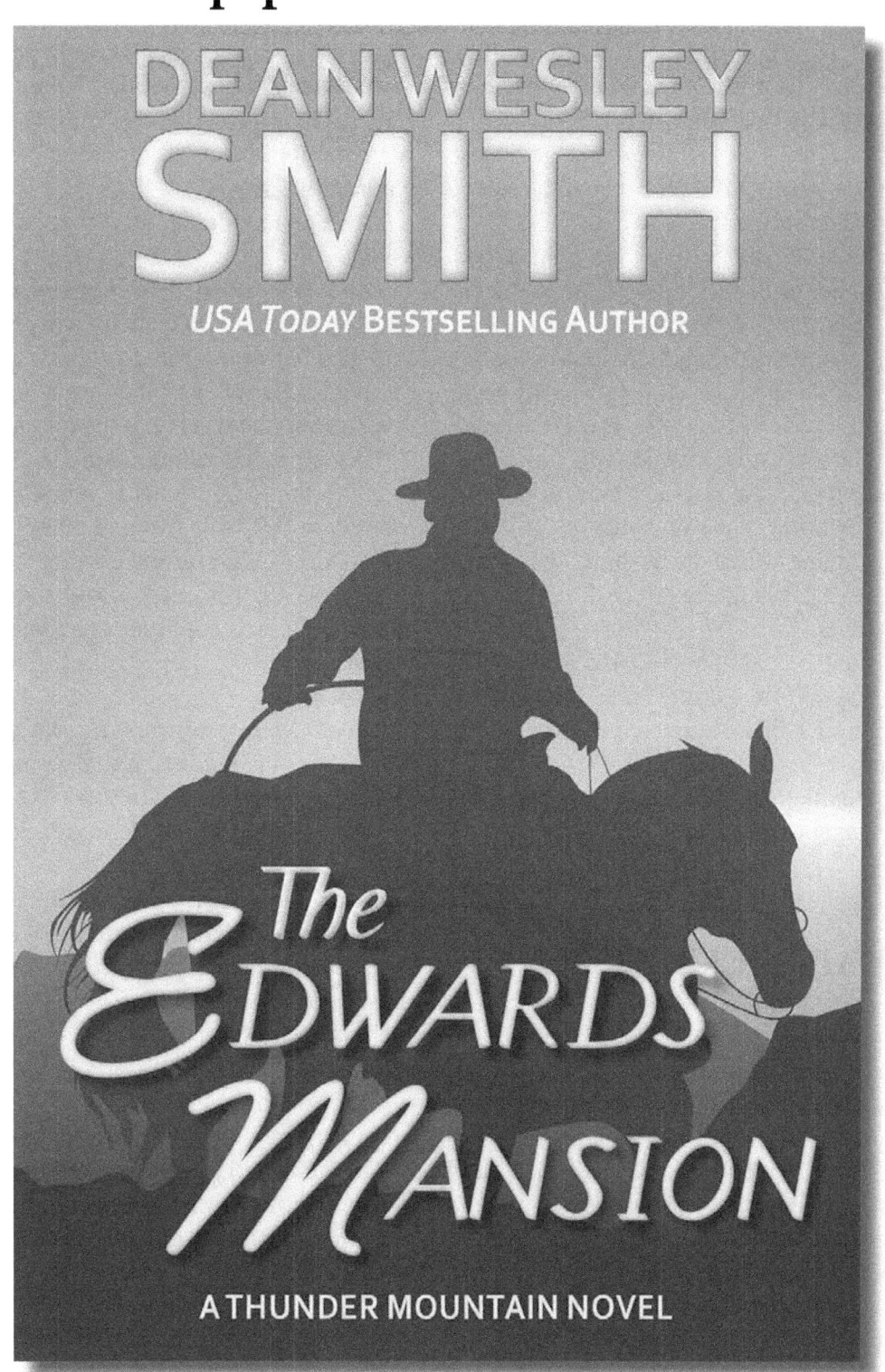

"So right now we are also existing outside of real time and real space?" Belle asked, glancing at Zane.

At that moment his stomach snapped down into a panic mode. He stood quickly, helping the surprised Belle to her feet as well. She managed to hold onto her sandwich in the process.

"We have to get back and get back fast," he said, stuffing the rest of the sandwich into his mouth.

"Why?" she said, as he helped her swing her pack back up on her shoulders.

"Because of what you said," Zane said, swinging his pack up onto his back. As soon as she was set, they headed back into the cavern they had come through. "We are existing outside of time and space here. Time does not exist in here."

"Oh, shit," she said softly, clearly understanding what he was thinking as they hit a fast pace and started back uphill into the caverns.

Zane just hoped beyond hope that they would find Bonnie and Duster just waiting for them, surprised at their quick return.

But he had a sinking feeling that was not going to be the case.

CHAPTER THIRTY

Unknown Time
Deep Inside the Crystal Caverns

WHEN THEY REACHED the archway between two of the caverns, Belle looked hard for the pile of dirt and the arrow they had made just an hour before. She couldn't see anything until Zane finally pointed at an area on the floor.

A very, very slight pile of dirt was there, not more than a slight bump now in the dirt, and their footprints of their walk in were gone.

"How long would it take for that to happen?" she asked as they went past.

"I honestly have no idea," Zane said. "These caverns might be resettling quickly or it might be a few thousand years of natural settlement."

"We're in trouble, aren't we?" Belle asked.

Zane only nodded and kept walking.

She stayed with Zane's fast pace as they headed through the caverns, taking out bottles of water as they went and not even trying to conserve at the moment.

Where it had taken them four hours to get to the main line of caverns, it only took them just over two and a half hours to get back to the starting cavern.

But as they headed across the large space, Belle was not liking at all what she was seeing.

Not at all.

There were only mounds where the table had been and their extra supplies.

Mounds covered in dust.

And the big metal door was mostly gone.

Zane took them straight to the table first. It had rotted away as had the wooden box, leaving only a pile of corroded and mostly destroyed pieces of equipment that had been the internal mechanism of the wooden box.

Their supplies were still there, but nothing more than a pile of rotted material and metal and plastic covered in dust.

Belle could feel the panic starting to climb up her throat and she took a deep breath and pushed it down.

"Got any idea how long it would take this to happen in this protected environment?" Belle asked, amazed her voice was even working at all.

"Thousands of years," Zane said flatly.

"We are so screwed," Belle said.

With that, Zane only nodded and turned to the door into the supply cavern.

The big metal door was nothing more than pitted rust and Zane easily kicked it down, sending dust swirling into the air.

They headed through the short tunnel and into the darkness of the supply cavern. No lights came up and both of them, using the light from the crystal cavern, dug out their flashlights and put on headlamps as well.

The smell in the big cavern was of rot. A thick smell as if the place had been closed up far, far too long.

Belle could tell that the condition of everything in here was as bad as the rotted table and supplies outside, if not worse. The supply tables were just piles of rubble, also covered in light dust.

With Zane leading, they picked their way toward the mine tunnel to the surface.

It had caved in a long, long time ago.

"Now we are really, really screwed," Belle said, staring at the solid wall of rock and dirt that blocked their path to the daylight beyond.

"Let's see exactly how long we were gone," Zane said, turning around and heading back into the supply cavern.

Belle remembered that Duster had shown them an atomic clock sealed in a vacuum and hidden in one rock wall. Zane went right for it and it took him only a moment to force open the hidden rock over the clock.

"Oh, shit," he said softly.

She looked in past him at the clock, and for a moment flat didn't even realize what she was seeing.

They had left the cavern in 1890. She was from 2020 and Zane was from 2120.

The clock said it was the year 3166. May 1st. Just before two in the afternoon to be exact.

She just kept staring at the numbers, standing with the man she had grown to love over the last month. After a moment the number started to sink in.

She laughed, because it was the only thing she could do. "Let me say this one more time. We are so screwed."

"Yeah, but we're both over a thousand years old, so what the hell," Zane said, shaking his head.

All she could do was laugh at that as well, which was only slightly better than just sitting on the floor and shaking.

CHAPTER THIRTY-ONE

May 1st, 3166
Inside the Crystal Caverns

AFTER SEEING THE atomic clock and what year and day it actually was for them, Zane took Belle's hand and they headed back into the light of the crystal cavern. They needed to preserve their batteries and they both needed to just get over the shock of what had just happened.

Belle had a smudge of dirt on the right side of her head and her hair was pulling loose from where she had it tied. After that cave, Zane knew they both smelled of rot and were both covered in dust and dirt.

They had basically been just handed a death sentence, and Zane knew it.

And he knew Belle knew it as well.

"Think it's a nice day outside right now?" Belle asked as they took another bottle of water and their last fresh beef sandwiches and sort of sat in the dirt and formed a picnic table with their packs about ten steps inside the crystal cavern.

The big open door to the cave beyond was like a scar in the beautiful wall of crystals.

"I'm going to pretend it's a nice day out there," Zane said, smiling at her.

"Think we might be able to dig ourselves out?" Belle asked.

"Maybe," Zane said. He had been calculating the chances of doing that after seeing the caved-in tunnel. "A miner dug his way in here in the 1870s, I sure don't see why we couldn't dig our way out."

Belle nodded. "I can hear the reservation in your voice in that sentence."

He smiled at her. "Getting to know me that much already, huh?"

She smiled back and he loved how she looked, even covered in dirt streaks. "I figure that since I'm going to be spending the rest of my life with you, I had better get to know you."

"I like the sounds of that," he said.

She laughed and then said, "Give, what is the reservation?"

"Digging is hard work and we're going to need water," Zane said, pointing to the packs and their only supplies that lay in the dirt between them. "The dig would be a race against our water supply."

Belle nodded, brushing her hair aside and leaving even more dirt smudges on the side of her face. "I figured as much. Maybe some of the old piping that Duster set up back in those restrooms still works. Or at least drips out some water of some sort that we can work with."

"We'll check it all out," Zane said, finishing off the last of his second beef sandwich of this adventure. He didn't give that much hope. But it was possible.

Anything, he supposed, was possible. But they were going to need a few very lucky breaks to survive this.

And if they did survive it, what was beyond that caved-in mine tunnel? Was anyone even still alive out there?

They sat for a moment in silence.

"Duster and Bonnie had a hunch this was going to happen, didn't they?" Belle asked.

"No," Zane said, realizing what she was asking and what he had known all along. "They knew it was going to happen."

"How do you know?" Belle asked, clearly stunned.

"Time travel," Zane said, gesturing to the remains of the old wooden table near one wall. They had been all the way to 2320, remember. They knew the future. They knew we were not a part of it, that we never returned."

"How do you know this?" Belle asked, a frown on her beautiful face.

"In my time, there were only 14 founders, not sixteen," Zane said. "And the genetics library was in your name, as if it was honoring you."

"Oh," Belle said. "So we were duped into sacrificing our lives for an experiment?"

Zane could hear the mounting anger in her voice, and he didn't blame her in the slightest. He wasn't happy in the slightest either. But anger wasn't going to help them now.

Clear heads when underground was the only thing that saved people, and right now they both needed to be thinking clearly.

"I don't think so," Zane said. "Remember, the point of all this was to find and stop a dictator who is using time travel to control the world in his time, and into his future."

"So," Belle said. "We discovered that no entrance could be found from the inside, and yet we can't relay that information back in time to help anyone. So they sacrificed us for no reason at all if they knew we were never coming back, except to learn that going into the distant caverns was a suicide mission."

Zane just could not believe that Bonnie and Duster would do that. It made no sense. He shook his head slowly, trying to make sense of what she had said.

"They wouldn't do that. And yet if they knew we would never return, they would have no reason to let us do this. Something is not making sense here."

"Yeah, like why did they want us out of the way?" Belle asked, her voice angry and biting.

"But they didn't," Zane said. "In fact, not once were we not treated as critical parts of the entire puzzle to save the mistakes they had started with time travel."

"Con artists are good at that," she said.

"But they gained nothing from conning us and sending us here," Zane said. "We're missing something. Something major."

"I sure hope you are right," Belle said.

But her voice did not sound like the anger was clearing in the slightest.

Then part of the answer dawned on him. "Remember, we took you forward and set your life with mine in 2120. Only two minutes and fifteen seconds are passing in 2120 for anything we do here."

She looked at him puzzled, slowly nodding. "So in essence, we can die and just end up fine and do this again."

Zane nodded. "And we can relay the information then."

She seemed to calm some with that. "Aren't we also anchored in 1900 and in 2020?"

"We are," he said. "So dying is not the end of the line. At some point we will just end up back in one of those places, unless leaving all time by going into that big cavern complex sort of messed us up."

"We won't know that for sure will we?" she asked.

"We could test it by dying," he said, looking in her dark eyes.

"I would rather not if we can help it," she said, smiling at him.

He agreed as well. The idea that there was a chance they might be anchored helped him some. Not a lot, but some. He just had a hard time believing that if they died here, they would end up gone only two minutes and fifteen seconds at some point along their last path.

So the plan was to not die.

He stood and offered her his hand, helping her to her feet.

"Do we put our packs inside or leave them here?" Belle asked.

"Just inside the door of the supply cavern," Zane said, picking his up. "Let's not take any chances with what little supplies we have being in some sort of accelerated time field."

She nodded and they moved their packs into the cavern, then turning on only their headlamps, they looked around the huge space of rotted wood and supplies.

Zane wanted to cover his nose from the intense smell of rot. He couldn't see anything of value.

Nothing.

Just too many years had passed.

"Didn't Duster have some other hidden rooms?" Belle asked. "He showed us one where he kept the money and gold. Maybe some supplies lasted better in those rooms."

"I doubt we'll be able to get into the money room, but worth a try," Zane said, and headed that way across the supply cavern, picking his way carefully through the rubble. No point in stepping on something rusty now and making his death even quicker.

The old money vault door was between the kitchen area and the entrance to the cavern, so they didn't have to go very far through the rubble.

At the cavern wall, where Duster had shown them where he stored money for trips into the past, Zane touched the two places that would unlock the large door and slide it aside.

He was expecting nothing to happen, but the rock slid aside without a sound.

Fresh-smelling and slightly cool air expelled from the vault room as the door opened. And a light came up, bright against the darkness.

"Wow, the room has been under pressure of some sort," Zane said.

Air continued to blow from the room outward so somewhere in here power was still working.

"Welcome back Dr. Russell and Dr. Logan," a voice said.

Zane knew that voice. It was Goldie's voice from their apartments in Boise.

"What the hell?" Belle asked. They both eased forward into the vault room.

The room was about the size of a decent bedroom, carved out of the rock, and lined on three sides with metal shelves that seemed to be in as good of shape as they had been on the day they were put in.

There was a lot of old bills stacked around the room on the shelves, and piles of gold in different forms. All the bills looked completely usable to Zane.

And there was no smell of rot in here at all.

How in the world was that even possible?

"Some of this money is from the last few hundred years," Belle said, picking up a strange-looking crisp bill and holding it in her hand. "Look at the date. And it's not rotted in any fashion."

Belle handed the bill to Zane. He just stared at it, not believing what he was holding.

Another light came on overhead and Goldie's voice said simply, "Please do not worry. I need to close the vault door and clean the air of the smell of rot and other contaminates before I can open the inner door. You can return to the cavern at any time."

Zane glanced back as the vault door slid shut behind them and sealed. He then could feel the air around them cycle quickly and even his clothes no longer smelled of the rot from that big cavern.

"Dry cleaning of the future," Belle said.

Then a slight feeling of movement happened and the entire room dropped deeper into the ground. After a moment, it stopped and the shelf directly in front of them slid aside and a large door opened into another hidden supply cavern beyond.

"How far did we drop, Goldie?" Zane asked.

"Five hundred and ten feet exactly," Goldie said.

"Oh, even in more trouble now," Belle said.

"You can return to the upper cavern any time you would like, Dr. Russell," Goldie said.

"Thank you, Goldie," Belle said, smiling at Zane.

Zane and Belle eased forward into the new cavern. It had lights hanging at regular intervals from the ceiling and tables with clothes on them. Zane could see a kitchen tucked off to one side. The entire cavern was even bigger than the rotted supply cavern they had just left.

It looked as if Bonnie and Duster hadn't forgotten them after all.

"Oh, thank heavens," Belle said, stepping forward into the large supply cavern. "Maybe we're not screwed just yet."

"We're in the year 3166," Zane said. "Remember?"

"And I don't feel a day over a thousand," Belle said.

Zane laughed. "I would say you don't look it either, but it's been a hard day."

"You are so going to pay for that," Belle said, laughing along with him.

And to Zane, after facing almost certain death trapped underground a few minutes before, laughing felt perfect.

PART FIVE
The Continuing Mission

CHAPTER THIRTY-TWO

May 1st, 3166
Inside the Crystal Caverns

BELLE COULDN'T BELIEVE the massive supply cavern that stretched out in front of them. Everything looked fresh and new and the air smelled wonderful and clean.

She and Zane stepped into the big room and the door to the vault and elevator behind them stayed open.

"There are bathrooms and showers in the back behind the kitchen," Goldie said, "and fresh clothes in the area with your names over them in the main supply area."

Belle walked with Zane into the supply area, their shoes making no sounds at all on the smooth stone floor. The cavern ceiling and walls were also stone and the ceiling was a good fifty feet over their heads. The overhead lights gave the place a warm feeling of very clear light, but nothing too bright.

One area of tables was marked Bonnie and Duster, another Dawn and Madison, and so on.

"That means they are coming here at times," Zane said, staring at the signs.

All Belle could do was nod at that.

There were eight different areas for all the founding couples, if she and Zane were included as founders, which they clearly seemed to be in this cavern.

There were tables and tables and racks of hanging clothes for them. From what Belle could tell, the clothes ranged from 1900 fashions to fashions and fabrics she had never seen before, and wondered if she could even wear.

Belle turned to Zane and smiled. "I have never been so happy to be wrong in my entire life."

"I'm just glad we don't have to dig that shaft out of here," Zane said.

Belle laughed, then said into the air, "Goldie, can you tell us where the rest of the founders are and when they will return."

"I am not aware of that information," Goldie said.

"Can you tell us what we are to do next?" Zane asked.

"I cannot, Dr. Logan," Goldie said. "My task is to see to your needs while you are in this location and maintain all the supplies in a fresh state. Nothing more."

"Thank you, Goldie," Belle said.

"You are more than welcome, Dr. Russell."

Belle stayed beside Zane as they walked around the cavern for a few more minutes, saying nothing, just trying to take in all the different areas. One entire area was filled with different devices, all clearly labeled for their time periods.

The table was like walking down a display of history, a large part of it they were not familiar with in any fashion.

Belle had no idea what some of the devices even pretended to be. And at one point around 2400, the technology seemed to regress a large amount before starting forward again.

"We have a lot to learn about our own history," Belle said.

"A vast amount," Zane said, staring at some of the devices from the 24th century.

"Goldie," Belle said into the air, "is there a form of library or learning area in this cavern?"

"There is, Dr. Russell. The door to that area is to the left of the kitchen as you face the bathrooms."

"Thank you, Goldie," Belle said.

"Well," Zane said, "it seems we have the ability to learn and we sure have the time."

Belle could only agree with that. But first she and Zane had to take care of themselves. She was feeling in shock from all of what happened today so far, and Zane had to be in the same shape.

"I'm going to take a shower," Belle said. "After that hike back here and the smell in that outer cavern, I really need to clear my head."

"While you do that," Zane said, "I'll look around a little. Then you can do the same while I shower."

She kissed him and then said, "A perfect plan."

She went over to their area and picked out a comfortable-looking pair of sweat pants and a soft sweatshirt from the 20th century and some slippers and then headed toward the bathrooms.

She normally would have offered to have Zane join her, but at the moment, she had a hunch they both needed some time.

She knew she did.

CHAPTER THIRTY-THREE

May 1st, 3166
Inside the Crystal Caverns

ZANE LET HIMSELF move slowly around the cavern, making note of the varied areas of supplies, just trying to grasp what he was seeing. Somehow, this cavern was being maintained in the year 3166 and he wasn't sure how or why, but he was glad it was.

There were even packaged supplies in the cabinets of the kitchen and Goldie said they were safe to eat.

He was about to head into the library area when he noticed something along one cavern wall near the library door.

There was an alcove there that had he and Belle's name over it on a silver plaque attached to the rock. In the carved alcove was a shelf with a box on it and blinking light near a white button.

There were seven other identical alcoves for the other founding couples along the wall, all identical except the blinking light and button.

At that moment Belle came out of the bathroom.

"Over here," he said.

She came over, looking refreshed and wonderful in the sweat pants and sweatshirt. She was using a dark towel to dry her hair and her skin looked slightly red as if she had scrubbed it harder than normal.

"Showers are wonderful," she said. "Once you figure out how to turn them on."

Then she saw what he was standing in front of. And the names over the other alcoves. "Any idea what this is all about?"

"Not a clue," Zane said. "I figured I would press that button when we were both here." He pointed at the green blinking light near a white button on a counter top fitted into the alcove.

"Go for it," Belle said.

Zane pushed it and then they both stepped back a half step as holographic images of Bonnie and Duster appeared. The images were about a foot tall and it looked like the two of them were standing on the counter beside the wooden box.

"Welcome back," Duster said.

"Yes, welcome," Bonnie said.

Zane was stunned. He didn't know what to do or say, so he simply took Belle's hand and they stood there, listening.

"Much has happened since you left," Duster said, "but now in the fight against the dictator who has terrorized the entire 23rd century using time travel, we need your help even more than before."

Bonnie nodded and Duster continued.

"We built this new hidden cavern eighty years after you vanished," Duster said, "In the year twenty-one hundred."

"It took us that long to finally figure out the math and what exactly happened to you," Bonnie said. "A full explanation of all that and what has happened, the entire lines of history since you vanished, is in the library area. Goldie can direct you to the right place."

"Of course, since we had traveled to the Step Three and Step Four at 2320," Duster said, "we knew you never returned, at least in the way we hoped you would return on the day you left. But we knew you would return here at some point in time first. We didn't know when, but this is why we built this cavern and have maintained it. And now we all continue to use it at times."

"So have we continued the fight," Bonnie said, "stopping the dictator in many millions of timelines, but he still exists in millions and millions more as we record this in 2364. We have been unable to find his original source of the crystals and close it. And we have been unable to find or stop the mathematicians that used our published work to help the dictator develop time travel with the crystals."

"We are continuing to look," Duster said, the small holographic image almost as intense as Duster in real life. "As we find more data, we update what we call our war room, which is through the library and behind a shelf of books there on mathematics. Pull the third book on the second shelf from the floor on the left to open it."

"So when you return," Duster said, "we need you to continue the fight to stop the dictator from whatever time you return in. Update the war room as you can in the last part of the 22nd century, at any point. All of us are doing that, pooling information as we find it."

"You will be a secret weapon," Bonnie said. "You will be attacking the sources of the dictator's power from the future."

Belle squeezed his hand at that and Zane nodded.

"We were forced to destroy the mine tunnel in 2364," Duster said. "The crystal in this box, this time you find yourself, is now your base time from the future. Once you have done what you can in the timeline in this crystal, return it to the main cavern outside the mine tunnel and remove another crystal from the wall from another area of the large cavern there and go back in that timeline."

"Do not contact us or return to the Warm Springs institute at any point in history," Bonnie said. "Live and exist under assumed names, different from timeline to timeline. Be cautious. Remember, our enemy, the enemy of all mankind, has time travel as well."

"Our goal is simple," Duster said. "Somehow get to the dictator's entrance into the crystal cavern before he is able to get to it and shut it off, so in that timeline and millions of others, he never finds the entrance."

"Your knowledge of the caverns should help with that now," Bonnie said.

"We hope it will," Duster said.

Zane wasn't so sure, but given enough time, he might be able to track the massive main caverns.

"In over three hundred timelines, we have killed the dictator when he was young in various accidents as he grew up," Bonnie said. "That saved billions of timelines from his reign as well."

Belle gasped at that, but Zane understood completely.

"And we are quickly working to scrub all our articles on time travel and the nexus of time and matter," Duster said. "Zane, since you are the only founder born after Bonnie and my first lifetimes, you should be able to stop numbers of articles as we publish them. Do what you can in any way you can to keep those articles from being printed without revealing yourself to us. We have left an entire list of the articles and their publication location and dates. We do not know which of our articles triggered the research by the dictator's people."

"But Belle will not be able to join you on those trips," Bonnie said. "It will vary the timeline too much to make the effort of value."

"So all this information and how to use the crystal in this box in front of you is in the library," Duster said. "Take your time, go slowly, plan your trips into the past."

"And be careful," Bonnie said.

"And when we have eliminated the dictator from all timelines," Duster said, we will update the war room in the year 2299, and then I hope we can all meet once again at the institute for a Christmas party in the year 2020."

"Until then," Bonnie said. "Take care and be careful."

Duster nodded and the two small holographic images vanished.

The button was no longer blinking and the silence in the cavern seemed suddenly very heavy.

Belle squeezed his hand and looked at him. "Seems we have things to do and an ongoing mission."

"It does," Zane said, nodding. "And it seems we have a way out of here after all."

He opened the wooden box to see a simple dial and some wires hooked up to a crystal tucked into the back of the box against the stone.

"You would think they could make a time travel machine look a little more modern by now," Belle said.

"As long as it works," Zane said. "I don't care what it looks like."

"That I agree with," she said, laughing as he closed the lid on the wooden box.

Then he quickly kissed her. "But before we do anything else, I need to take a shower and we need to get something to eat."

"I'll bring you some fresh clothes," she said. "And I promise to behave myself."

"What's the fun in that?" he asked, laughing as he turned and headed for the bathroom.

And it turned out that she offered to scrub his back, and he had accepted, and as far as he was concerned, that was heaven in any century.

CHAPTER THIRTY-FOUR

December 31st, 3166
Inside the Crystal Caverns

SHE AND ZANE had spent almost a month, mostly in the library, trying to get updated on the huge battle they were involved in. The library was perfectly named. It was a large cavern with ten-foot-tall shelves jammed with books from various centuries. Most of the aisles were so close together, it was almost impossible to walk through the stacks without turning sideways.

One area near the door was filled with massive wooden tables and the stone floor in that area had been covered in a thick carpet. There were reading chairs, a couple of old brown couches that looked to be from the 20th century, and a fake fireplace that imitated flame and even put out a little heat.

It was, by far, the most comfortable place in the caverns.

She had taken over three large wooden tables for her research and he had taken over three for his. Both tables had numbers of computer-like terminals on them that also accessed large data bases stored somewhere in the rocks.

They slept every night in one of the two bedrooms off the kitchen and ate decent packaged foods that mostly tasted of nothing in particular.

But most of the time they were in the library.

The war room was just a stark stone room with the walls covered in vast computer-generated images that showed timelines in representations of millions in a single line.

The timelines looked to Belle like massive trees branching out. Clearly Bonnie and Duster and their incredible math skills had been able to trace major timelines that broke off from events through history.

Over half the room had the timelines colored in green, but almost half the room showed red indicating they were timelines that the dictator still functioned.

Belle had not liked going into that war room. It was flat too depressing to realize that every thin line was thousands and thousands of world where millions suffered and eventually the world was destroyed.

After a month, they had decided to make their first trip back in time.

The crystal in their booth jumped them back into the year 2299. That was the year that Duster had said they would update the war room if the dictator had been defeated.

No one else was there. They had spent ten days studying the war room to discover more updates from the other founders. The dictator was still in control of a vast amount of the world in a vast amount of timelines. And his control extended forward for over a century until almost all of humanity was destroyed in those timelines.

Most of the red lines just ended like trees cut off in their growth.

Zane said there might be a way to really stop the dictator in a more effective way instead of working timeline cluster to timeline cluster, as the rest were doing, but he said it was so crazy, he didn't want to talk about it.

So they decided to jump back to their future time. They both felt safer there. There the old mine was sealed up and the deep chamber very, very well hidden under the rubble of the old one.

They had left no sign or evidence they had been in 2299. Both of them, for some reason, felt that was very important.

They didn't want the other founders to know they had yet returned in any future time.

They spent almost another six months in the research library in 3166, going over every detail of centuries of battles with the dictator through thousands and thousands of timelines.

Killing the dictator when he was young had worked in many, many timeline clusters, but he had set up guards on himself and his family, so doing that no longer worked.

So when they returned to 3166, they both first returned to focusing on what Bonnie and Duster had wanted them to focus on. She went looking for genealogical clusters of lines starting suddenly to find possible crystal cavern openings.

Zane went back to looking for more openings through research in ground structure and known cave entrances.

Both of them were experts in doing research, and they both knew how to do it. So the days went easily, and Belle enjoyed Zane's company a great deal. She could never have imagined feeling so comfortable locked underground with another person. Yet not once during those six months did she feel she needed to get away from him.

In fact, the longer they were together, the more it felt like they just were together.

They were a team.

On the research side, Zane had spent most of his time poring over geological maps along the 42nd parallel and any historical reference to large mining operations along that line.

She had buried herself in searching for clusters of genealogical starts.

What she had found bothered her more than she wanted to admit. All of the clusters of genealogical lines like hers that just started cold had been found and already covered by the other founders.

And none of them were near any logical entrance to the crystal caverns. The clusters seemed to always come from two people as hers came from Dawn and Madison. And most could be explained away by a few dozen dictator's loyalists who had backgrounds in the dictator's time.

So the genealogical side was flat a dead end on tracking where a new crystal entrance might be.

In fact, Zane said to her when she told him that he could find no other possible crystal mine entrance.

Period.

So on New Year's Eve, the two of them sat at the wooden table in the kitchen munching on popcorn and drinking hot chocolate and talking about their findings.

"I'm coming to only one true result," Zane said, shaking his head and staring into her eyes with those wonderful dark eyes of his.

"There is no other entrance to the crystal caverns." Belle said.

Zane nodded. "There might be in some distant and extreme other timelines, but in any timeline that we would recognize, that mine shaft up there is it."

"You sure?" she asked.

"I am," Zane said. "Completely sure. All the other crystal caverns are far too removed in distance and time and timelines from the surface of a world we might know, even accounting for any of those side rooms getting too close to the surface."

"So how did the dictator, or someone who knows him in 2320, get into the mine?"

Zane shook his head. "I honestly don't know, but Bonnie and Duster clearly had an inkling of that being possible when they destroyed the mine tunnel. But too late at that point."

Belle had to agree with that. There must have been a period of time in the early 2300s that they let the security of the mine lag. Maybe for decades. Destroying the mine tunnel above could have only meant that Duster and Bonnie were worried about the caverns already being discovered as well.

"So what do we know about the dictator?" Zane asked.

Belle just shrugged. "The man and his family were nothing special. He simply gained power through the normal political process and then in the early 24th century, he became President of the United States and from 2320 forward he never let go of power. It became clear in short order to Duster and Bonnie and the rest of the original founders that the man was using time travel to control those around him by various means."

Zane nodded, so Belle went on after munching on some popcorn first.

"The dictator basically annexed the rest of the world with threats and annihilation over the next forty years after he controlled this country and ruled the world with force and terror for over a hundred years, never seeming to age much at all when he was seen, until a major war and following plague simply destroyed most of the human population.

"So it's this mine that is the problem," Zane said. "And Duster and his family finding it in the first place."

Belle nodded. "And without seeing the mine, Bonnie told me that she and Duster would have never started working on their time travel theories."

Zane nodded and the two of them sat there in silence.

"You have an idea, don't you?" Belle asked.

Belle had a hunch she knew what he was going to say, but she didn't like it, so she would rather let Zane say it out loud.

Zane nodded. "I do, and because we are where we are at, we are the only two who can pull it off. We find a timeline where he was cleared out and use that as a base in the cavern above."

Belle nodded.

"And then we jump to a timeline where he has not been cleared out. Then we jump back and destroy this mine before Bonnie and Duster can see it. We set a timer so we can get out before we also vanish in that timeline."

Zane had been right. She hated the idea. Because without the mine, Zane would live his life a hundred years in her future and she would never meet him.

And that she could no longer imagine.

But she could also no longer imagine letting a single man destroy humanity in millions of timelines.

CHAPTER THIRTY-FIVE

December 31st, 3166
Inside the Crystal Caverns

IT HAD TAKEN Zane a few minutes to fully explain his plan to her. Since the dictator had been stopped in so many timelines, Zane had no intention of not being with Belle.

But just not in every timeline.

Not in the timelines where the dictator ruled.

Zane had finally convinced her and the two of them had spent the next four days learning how to use the explosives that Duster and Bonnie had stored in the cave. Zane had worked with explosives before and timed switches to open up some caves, so he knew enough to just be dangerous.

But they were both great at studying something, and with Belle double and triple checking him every step of the way, in a few days he felt comfortable with the idea of handling enough explosive power to completely bring down the mine tunnel so that no one would dig it out again.

And he figured if they destroyed the mine in 1778, right after Duster and

Bonnie had put in all the security, there would be no reason for any of Duster's relatives to open the played out mine again.

But the more they worked on his plan, the more Zane didn't like it.

Belle even said one day over lunch that she felt the focus of the founders in this fight had been all wrong. They had assumed that the dictator had found another opening. And they had assumed the mine here was impossible to both find and get into.

And that their articles were to blame.

Zane had agreed that he too thought the founders' focus had been wrong. Blowing up that mine tunnel was just another path.

So they both decided they would step back and look at everything again and spend a few weeks, since they had all the time they needed, to come up with a better idea.

It was a week later that Belle finally brought up a better plan.

And a more logical explanation of what had happened.

They had just finished lunch and Belle had asked him to look at something in her research in the library.

She brought up a screen on her large computer terminal among piles of books on one of her tables showing basically a family tree of the dictator.

Zane was surprised as he studied the very complex family tree illustrated on the screen. "You have all this on the man?"

Belle nodded. "The work that Bonnie and Duster had the institute do on this project is stunning in how clear and complete it is back through history."

"The dictator himself wouldn't even know some of this," Zane said, staring at the screen.

"Not unless he would have been studying his own family for decades," Belle said. "And then had the resources that Bonnie and Duster and the institute put together over a full century of work after we left."

Zane was starting to catch on, but nodded that Belle go on.

"We need to assume the dictator has all his immediate family in history now covered," Belle said, "but we can also assume that there is only so far he can go back in time in any crystal without ending up in the crystal cavern above and risking exposure."

She drew a line on the family tree around 2220. "I want to assume that it was the expansion of people who knew about the institute of Step Three that caused him to discover the crystals."

Zane nodded. "So he might have gotten the crystals he ended up using from the institute instead of the mine above."

"Exactly," Belle said. "Those crystal rooms for travel are huge and hold thousands of crystals and all it would take would be one person not happy with the institute in 2220 to replace a real crystal with a dummy crystal and take out the real one."

"I tried to sneak back in time by simply using a crystal clear to the back of one room," Zane said. "It didn't work, but I sure thought it did."

"Exactly," Belle said.

"And they wouldn't need to have a mathematics genius," Zane said. "All they would have to do would be to smuggle out a crystal and one box from the back of one room and a few crystals."

"Exactly," Belle said. "Replace a real box with a fake one, then use the time travel device for some personal gain and have it eventually fall into the wrong hands. The dictator's hands after he became president."

"Security can always be breached," Zane said, nodding. "That makes a ton more sense than finding and then breaching this mine above us."

"It does," Belle said.

"So what are you thinking?" Zane asked.

She looked away from her computer terminal and smiled at him and it was the first real smile she had given him since discovering they were actually safe in 3166.

"We don't know who will be the thief," Belle said, "but we can go back to almost the start of the institute and make sure that Bonnie and Duster and Director Parks are alert and can catch the person."

"That will stop a lot of the dictator's timelines," Zane said, "but not all of them."

"I know," Belle said. "So let's assume the dictator can't go back any farther than one hundred years, since Bonnie and Duster designed those devices in the institute to hold at that."

She drew a hundred year line across the dictator's family tree.

Zane liked the look of that line. In fact, he liked it more than he wanted to admit.

"To kill any plant or tree completely," Belle said, "we need to kill it at its roots. If we do that, combined with making sure that Bonnie and Duster and Director Parks increase security, I think we take the dictator out of all the timelines."

She circled on the screen one name right at the bottom of the family tree.

Zane stared at the name. Albion Jones.

"If we don't allow Albion Jones to marry miss Edda Seavy in Moscow, Idaho, in June of 1902, this tree dies."

Belle killed the connection between the two people on the tree showing that

they got married and had seven children and the entire family tree vanished.

Zane stared at that and then kissed Belle, long and hard.

And she kissed him back.

Maybe, just maybe, they had a way out of all this.

CHAPTER THIRTY-SIX

July 18th, 2020
Boise, Idaho

STOPPING THE MARRIAGE between Albion Jones and Edda Seavy had turned out to be very, very easy for two people with more than enough time to spend.

Albion was from the Twin Falls area of Idaho in the southern part of the state, while Edda was a local farm girl from a town called Palouse near Moscow in the northern part of the state.

With some research, Belle and Zane had discovered that Albion had sent out applications for three schools and been accepted to all three, picking the engineering department at the new University of Idaho land grant college in the farm community of Moscow, Idaho, over a similar acceptance to an engineering school in Corvallis, Oregon.

That was where he met Edda.

So Zane came up with the idea of just going back and living in Twin Falls as young Albion grew up and seeing what they could change in his life. It had seemed simple and easy because Zane honestly didn't much like the idea of hurting anyone and doubted that either of them could do that.

"We would have to be a married couple," Belle had said.

"I like the sounds of that," Zane had said and Belle had kissed him for that, which he had enjoyed as well.

They had returned in time to 1890. Moving as a young married couple to Twin Falls, Idaho, they had gotten into the small rural community there. Even though they had brought more than enough money from the future, they pretended to be just regular folk.

Belle had hated the clothes of the time, but they had taken enough modern underwear and supplies to help them make the transition to living in the past.

Over the next twelve years, Zane had taken a job as a mail carrier, which he honestly liked. He liked the people and the job gave him time to learn about the time and to think.

Belle had become a teacher, which she said she enjoyed as well. They both had become friends with the Jones family and watched young Albion come up through school.

Belle, when she had Albion in her class, talked up the Oregon schools and Zane had ended up delivering the Jones' mail.

There just was no way of telling that such a young family and a nice young man could be a distant and critical relative to the worst criminal in all time. Albion and his family were very nice, down-to-earth people who wanted their oldest son to do well.

The entire time Zane and Belle were there in Twin Falls, both of them were on high alert to any signs of anyone else from the future being around the young man. Zane was very glad they saw nothing.

Albion wanted to attend the Oregon school by the time he applied for college, but had still sent out applications to the same three schools as he originally had done.

Zane made sure that the acceptance from the University of Idaho in Moscow never arrived at the Jones' home.

And then he and Belle made sure that the Jones family had enough money

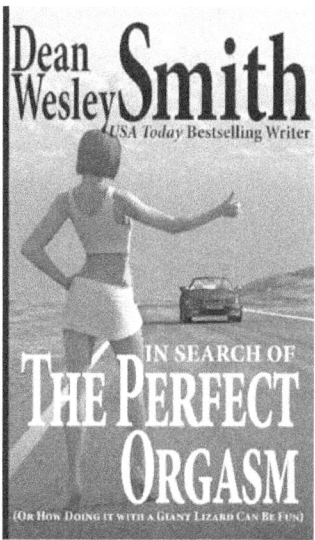

to get Albion to Oregon by sponsoring a fake college scholarship that Albion won.

Zane delivered that letter as well.

Zane and Belle stayed in Twin Falls and in their jobs until Albion Jones graduated from college, married a childhood sweetheart from Twin Falls, and settled down.

Belle had very, very much enjoyed their time living as a married couple in the past and told Zane that a few times the last year they were there.

Zane had to admit, he had enjoyed it as well, and one night he mentioned that they should think of doing this in their real time.

Belle had loved the sound of that. And he had been rewarded in wonderful ways that night in their featherbed for his suggestion.

Then, after Albion was settled in safely in his new life, Belle and Zane had said goodbye to their friends in Twin Falls and headed back to the mine.

They had planned on going to the war room in 2299 to see what their actions had done.

But when Zane unplugged one wire from the box in the crystal cavern, things got very, very strange.

CHAPTER THIRTY-SEVEN

June 16th, 2020
Boise, Idaho

FOR A MOMENT, Belle found herself touching the wooden box in the crystal cavern, then a shimmering started like heat waves rolling over a desert.

But there was no heat, just shimmering, as if her eyes were playing a trick on her and everything around her was shifting.

She then found herself beside Zane touching the box that was in the alcove in the hidden cave in 3166.

But the shimmering continued.

She then found herself touching the wooden box with Bonnie and Duster in the crystal cavern again.

And then, finally, she found herself touching the wooden box in the Step One crystal room in the institute.

And then finally she found herself sitting drinking a Diet Coke in the living room cavern of the institute.

Then slowly the shimmering stopped, vanishing as if nothing had happened.

Zane sat beside her, also sipping on a Diet Coke.

She knew the date was June 16th, 2020.

The date that Bonnie and Duster and Dawn and Madison and Parks had told Belle and Zane about the dictator for the first time.

It was in this very meeting.

But how was this possible?

Belle remembered how she had been recruited for the institute, but without any mention of the dictator. And how she had gone with Zane into the past and then into the future.

And then she remembered the last week of learning everything about the institute and getting to know and care for Zane.

But she also remembered clearly living with Zane now for years in the past, and living in a secret chamber under the old cavern, and going into the massive crystal cavern and everything.

She remembered both timelines completely.

How was that possible?

She glanced at Zane who was sitting beside her, blinking.

He looked completely stunned and younger than the face she had grown used to looking at and kissing in Twin Falls, Idaho.

Bonnie and Duster both sprang to their feet and both were smiling so hard, they both looked like they might hurt themselves. They hugged each other and then danced, actually danced, swinging each other around and around.

Clearly they remembered both timelines as well for some reason.

"Holy shit!" Duster said, finally stopping and staring at Belle and Zane. "You two did it!"

Belle felt too shocked to even stand up, and beside her Zane clearly looked shocked as well.

Dawn and Madison and Director Parks just sat in their chairs looking stunned at the outburst from Bonnie and Duster.

"Bonnie and I remember as well," Duster said, "because we were touching the wooden box when all four of us went back."

"Did we just have another major timeline shift?" Madison asked. "And I was left out again?"

"A monster," Bonnie said, laughing. "Bigger than you can ever imagine."

"I'm remembering two different timelines," Zane said after Duster finally calmed down enough to sit back down.

Both Duster and Bonnie nodded and just kept smiling like children given a huge piece of candy.

Belle managed to somehow take a deep breath. She really was with Zane and she really was in the living room a week after she and Zane had jumped to establish her in Step Two.

She remembered falling for Zane in the front room of the institute just a week before, and she remembered their first trip into the past where they almost froze walking out to Warm Springs Avenue and back.

And it seemed that the last week they were still just getting to know each other, being careful about what they said and so on.

But she also remembered the years living with him as a married couple in the small rural farming town of Twin Falls, Idaho, and falling in love with him, and so much more.

"Only the four of us will ever remember the dictator," Duster said.

"Thankfully," Bonnie said, nodding.

"We need a few huge drinks and a long explanation," Duster said, "and how you completely stopped the dictator in all timelines."

"The dictator!" Director Parks shouted. "What dictator? What the hell is going on here?"

Belle laughed, slowly letting this new reality sink in.

"You have some security issues in the institute in the future, Director Parks," Zane said, smiling.

Belle laughed. "Major ones."

Director Parks opened his mouth, but nothing came out.

Duster looked shocked. "That's how the dictator got his crystals? From here, right under our noses?"

"And we think someone also took a machine," Belle said. "As President of the United States, the dictator just ended up with them, more than likely not knowing where they came from, but eventually figuring out how they worked."

"So how did you stop the dictator?" Bonnie asked.

"Would someone please tell us what dictator?" Dawn and Madison asked at the same time.

Duster waved his hand. "We'll explain the thousands of years of battles that just ended."

"Thousands of years?" Director Parks asked. Belle could see the shock and puzzlement in his face.

"Boy, you weren't kidding about major timeline shift," Madison said.

"I want to know how you two did it," Duster said, staring at Belle and then at Zane.

"My memory tells me I just didn't deliver a piece of mail," Zane said.

And with that, Belle could only laugh at the shocked looks on everyone's face.

Zane reached over and took her hand and then looked at her directly. "You remember what we were talking about in Twin Falls the year before we left?"

She smiled. "I sure do."

"So would you marry me?" he asked. "I think this time is about as real as it's going to get."

"After all those years of living in sin with me," she said, "I think it is about time you asked."

"I take that as a yes?" he said, laughing.

"Yes," she said.

Then she kissed him.

And he kissed her back.

She didn't care at all that the founders of the institute were just sitting there staring at them, three stunned, the other two smiling and laughing.

She planned on spending an eternity with Zane, and since they already had been all over a dozen centuries and had saved millions of lives in millions of timelines, they deserved a little time for a honeymoon.

And if their honeymoon lasted a few lifetimes, that was fine with her as well.

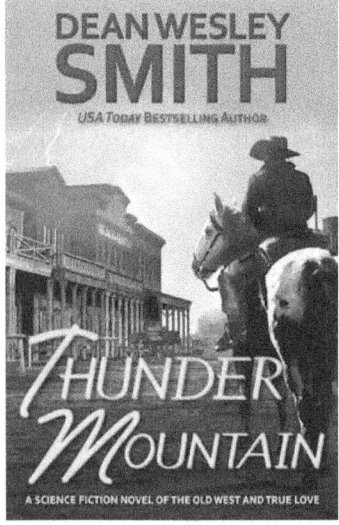

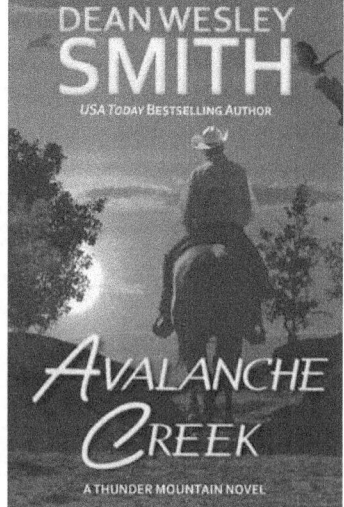

The First Three Thunder Mountain Novels
Available at your favorite booksellers.

Coming Next Issue in Smith's Monthly
A return to the Cold Poker Gang
in a brand new mystery novel.
CALLING DEAD

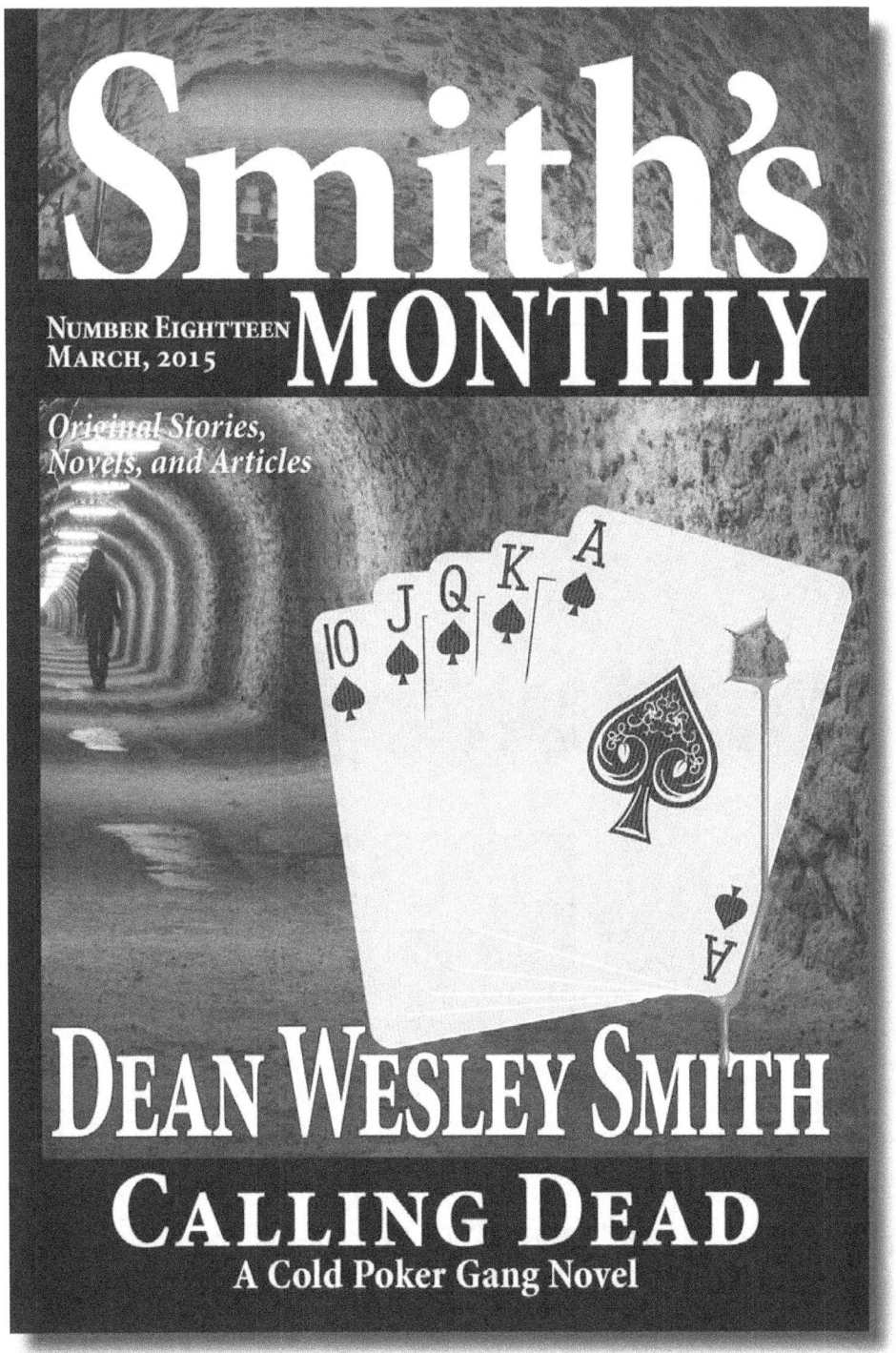

#1... October 2013

#2... November 2013

#3... December 2013

#4... January 2014

#5... February 2014

#6... March 2014

#7... April 2014

#8... May 2014

#9... June 2014

#10... *July 2014*

#11... *August 2014*

#12...*September 2014*

#13...*October 2014*

#14...*November 2014*

#15...*December 2014*

The First Fifteen Issues of Smith's Monthly!!!

Subscribe Now and start with any issue.
All issue are available from all your favorite booksellers
in trade paper and electronic editions.

www.smithsmonthly.com

Thank You!!

Walter White Cat and I would like to thank
the following wonderful people who support my blog
and my work through Patreon.
Your support is very important to me.
Thanks!

Rob Cornell
Erick Lindman
Christopher Ridge
Miguel Angel Alonso Pulido
Ryan M. Williams
Jacob Proffitt
Ryan Whiteside
Marian Goldeen
John Connelly
Gary Speer
Megan Bryce
Michelle Tatam
Robin Brande
J.R. Murdock
Kathleen McClure
Michael Kelberer
Gunnar Gunderson
F.I. Goldhaber
Mary Jo Rabe